Wicked Clow.   ......,

by

Sara Bourgeois

Chapter One

A piercing scream from the backyard nearly had me drop the birthday cake I'd spent the better part of the morning perfecting. Fortunately, my mom and Thorn had been more than happy to keep Laney happy and entertained while I sifted, mixed, baked, frosted, and finally... decorated.

I didn't know what Laney would want, so I adorned it with a fondant unicorn and some sparkles. The unicorn had taken some work and more than one attempt. It was okay, though, because I'd happily eaten all the failures.

I'd loved unicorns when I was little, so I went with it. When I heard the shriek, I set it down as gently as I could, and with my heart threatening to burst out of my chest, ran out the back door.

"What is it?" I yelled as I kicked the door open and jumped out onto the patio, like I was some sort of ninja with the power to defeat a horde of evil forces. But could you blame me? My baby was out there. If there was danger, I'd ninja it to the best of my ability. Fortunately, everyone kept their eyes focused on the source of the screaming and hadn't noticed my grand entrance. Everyone but my husband. Of course, he'd been watching the door for me.

Thorn's face turned bright red and he started laughing hysterically at the sight of my fierce warrior moves. I looked around just in time to see Amanda Lee scoop up her kid and run toward the driveway. Like, she booked it. I had no idea she could even move that fast.

"What is it?" I asked again. "What the heck is going on?"

My eyes scanned the small crowd of partygoers gathered in our backyard. My Mom was holding Laney and stifling a laugh, but she appeared to be chuckling at Amanda's antics. The baby was fine, so I was thoroughly confused.

Thorn made his way over to me. "Honey, the clown is here," he said warily. His laughter faded as the realization set in. The realization that he was about to have to spend an hour with Chuckles the Happy Party Clown. Apparently, he hadn't been joking about clowns making him uncomfortable.

"Is that what all that was about?" I asked.

"Apparently, that Amanda chick is more afraid of clowns than I am," he said. "She screamed when he came around the corner. Did you see how fast she ran out of here?"

"I did." And it was my turn to chuckle. "I hope she brought a gift. Who invited her anyway?"

"Kinsley, be nice," Thorn chastised. "Ugh, I think I need to go too, though. My blood pressure is shooting up." I noticed that lines of sweat had broken out above his brow and lips.

"What? Really? It's your daughter's first birthday, Thorn," I said. "Why don't you try a beer? I could grab you one after I get the cake."

"I've been here for most of it," he protested. "It's just that... I don't... I'm so sorry, honey."

"Do they really bother you that much?" I asked. "I shouldn't have hired him. It just seemed like he'd be good at distracting these young kids. Plus..."

"I should have said something when you were planning. I knew you were trying to egg me on, and I should have said something. Stupid masculine pride," he said. "I really thought I'd be okay, though. It's been a long time since I had any kind of incident with a clown."

"There have been incidents?" I asked.

"Well, I'm not afraid of clowns out of nowhere," Thorn answered. "I'll tell you about it later, okay? He's looking at me." He shivered, and I realized that he was having a serious reaction to the clown.

Thorn was a brave, stoic man most of the time, but I think I'd found his kryptonite. I could tell he was straining to maintain his calm. I knew then I would put an end to it. The kids weren't paying any attention to Chuckles anyway. They hadn't gotten excited about his arrival at all. Not one laugh.

"I'm going to pay him and ask him to go," I said. "This is my fault. None of the kids are even looking at him anyway."

"You don't have to do that," Thorn said. "I could go in the house and watch her blow out the candles from the kitchen. Or I could stand at the back of the yard."

I laughed, but then I felt terrible. He was really afraid. I'd never seen Thorn get that rattled. "You will do no such thing," I said. "I will pay him and send him on his way. Then we can do the cake."

"Thank you, sweetie," Thorn said.

"But at some point, you have to tell me this story. It's got to be good," I said.

"I will," Thorn said with an uncomfortable laugh. He rubbed the back of his neck nervously and then joined my parents with his back turned to the clown.

I'd hired Chuckles from a website where you could book party entertainment. I should have known better when he was listed right along with stripper nurses and a potty-mouthed singing gorilla. On second thought, I would have been better off with the gorilla.

Anyway, the guy reeked of beer. I could smell it on him when I was still several feet away. As I got closer, it became obvious he had bloodshot eyes as well.

He almost said something as I approached, but I put my hand up to stop him. "I'm calling you a cab. You're lucky I'm going to pay you."

"Fine by me," he slurred. "I hate doing these stupid kiddy parties anyway."

"Excuse me?" I couldn't believe what I'd heard, but then I realized I totally could. The guy was sloshed at a baby's birthday party. Nothing he said should have shocked me. "You know what, never mind.

Meet me around front, I'll get your money and call you a cab."

"I got my car," he protested.

"And my husband is the sheriff," I said and pointed toward Thorn. "You so much as breathe in the direction of your car, and I'll make sure you go to jail. And if you make my husband leave his child's first birthday party to haul your sorry butt to jail, me not paying you will be the best part of your day."

"Are you threatening me, lady?"

"I'm making you some very solemn promises," I retorted. "Now, meet me around the front of the house, and I'll pay you."

"Fine," he said and waved me off.

I went in through the back door and grabbed the envelope with Chuckles' check in it off the counter. When I booked him, I thought I'd be able to pay online. Turned out to be a good thing that I couldn't. I had to wonder if they'd had problems with their entertainers in the past.

Out front, I found Chuckles sort of teetering on the bottom step leading onto the porch. "Whoa, you should sit down," I said.

He started to try to walk up the stairs, and I watched him nearly fall backwards. "Maybe I'll just sit here," he finally said.

Chuckles turned around and plopped down on the second step. I was glad he came to that conclusion on his own because I was about to suggest it. At least I didn't have to argue with the drunk clown in my front yard.

"Here's your fee," I said and handed him the envelope.

He nearly dropped it. "How long until the taxi gets here?"

"You didn't call one?" I asked. "I guess maybe I said I'd do it. I didn't know you'd actually... You know what? Never mind. I'm calling someone right now."

I got my phone out of my pocket and called the only taxi company in Coventry. It wasn't really a company per se, but more of a retired gentleman that did it to make a little extra money.

"Teddy's Terrific Taxi," he answered.

"Teddy, this is Kinsley over at Hangman's House, I was wondering if you were available to pick someone up?" I asked.

"Oh, I've got some time," he said. "Can't be too long, though. I'm taking a gal into the city later this afternoon. To the airport. I imagine that will take up most of my time. Who is it?"

"Okay, so I hired a party clown for my daughter's birthday," I said. "And he's a drunk fool. I was hoping you could come get him off my front porch so I can go back to my daughter's birthday."

"I am not a drunk fool," Chuckles sloshed.

I really wished I could turn him into a goat. Instead, I just glared at him until he looked away in shame and went back to my call.

"A drunk clown you say?" Teddy snickered. "I haven't gotten that call for a while."

"I'm sure there's a story behind that. I know it's a lot to ask and probably outside your purview."

"Nonsense," Teddy said. "I've handled my share of drunk fools in my life. I'll be there in ten minutes or less."

"Thank you so much," I said. After I hung up with Teddy, I turned my attention back to Chuckles. Man, I wished I remembered the guy's real name. I wasn't going to ask. My hope was to never see him again anyway. "I'm going back in the house. Don't move."

"Do you have any coffee?" Chuckles asked and then rubbed his temples. Some of the white paint on his face came off on his red gloves.

I let out a deep sigh before retreating into the house. I wasn't going to make the guy a pot of coffee, so instead I grabbed a Coke from the fridge. Once I had that, I picked up my wallet and headed out to the porch.

"Here. This is the best I'm willing to do," I said and handed him the soda. Next I took money for Teddy out of my wallet and handed him that too. "This is for Teddy. I'll call him later, and if I find out that you stiffed him on the tip, I'll find you."

"This is a generous tip," Chuckles said after quickly counting the money.

"Don't even think about it," I said. "You're lucky this sorry little encounter is ending this way. I really should have had my husband, or one of his deputies, haul your sorry butt to jail. You're lucky that it's my daughter's birthday and all I want is to go back to that. If you think you're getting a tip for trying to ruin the birthday party, you're crazy. Now, just sit there and wait for Teddy. I have to go back."

I didn't give Chuckles the chance to say anything else, but I did look out the front window when I got inside. He was sitting there on the step sipping the Coke I'd given him. Satisfied, I returned to the party.

The unicorn cake was a hit with the guests. Laney's eyes lit up when she saw it, but she loved the little pink smash cake I made even more.

Thorn took video of Laney smashing her cake to bits while I got a few presents ready out in the yard. Lots of people had brought gifts, but we were only going to help her open a few at the party. I knew a one-year-old would get overwhelmed with the mountain of gorgeously wrapped white, pink, and yellow packages.

As I was crouched down setting up, someone I didn't expect walked through the back door and onto the patio. "Annika and Uncle Gunner," I said and stood up. "Wow. What a lovely surprise!"

A second later, my mom and dad were out of their chairs and standing in front of my aunt and uncle on the patio. I cleaned Laney off while they all shared hugs and some tears.

"Annika," I said as I brought Laney close to her, "it's so good that you're here."

"I hope you don't mind that I crashed the party," she said and blushed a little. Uncle Gunner put his arm around her waist and she stood up a little taller. I was so happy to see that they were in a good place together.

"Of course not," I said. "I would have invited you, but we haven't heard from you guys in a while."

"I'm sorry about that," Annika said and then bit her bottom lip.

"Nonsense," I replied. "No apologies today. You're here, and that's all that matters."

I felt a tap on my shoulder and turned around to find Amelda standing behind me. She wasn't normally one to stand back and wait for someone to move out of her way, but even with the youth spells covering all of us, the years had begun to get after her. Judging by the look in her eyes in that moment, it could have been Annika's absence that caused her aging, though.

Most people knew that there was a bit of a competition between Annika and my father as to who was Amelda's favorite grandchild. Annika's estrangement from the family had caused Amelda immense pain. She'd borne it well. Amelda was tough as nails, but I could see her prickly exterior faltering. I stepped out of the way.

"Grandma," Annika barely choked out.

"Hush now," Amelda said with a level of tenderness I didn't think she possessed. She pulled Annika into her arms, and they stood there for a moment.

Meanwhile, Laney reached out for Uncle Gunner and squealed for him to take her. I was surprised, but Gunner looked shocked.

"I think she likes you," I said.

He studied Laney for a moment and then took her from me. Even nearing his seventies, Gunner was still a huge, strapping man. But he melted like butter left out in the sun when Laney cuddled up against him.

"I think I have a new friend," he beamed with pride.

"I'd say so," I said with a laugh. "We were about to open some gifts. I think she'd like to stick with you, if that's all right?"

"Of course," Gunner said.

"Wait, before we get to the party gifts, I have something I'd like to give her," Annika said.

I didn't seen any gift in her hands, and at the time, I didn't know about the giving ceremony, so I was a little confused. There had been a ritual when I was born where all of the aunties gave me some sort of power or ability. My Mom never actually told me about it, though.

There were some non-witches around with their kids, so Annika kept it vague. "I give baby Laney the gift of tolerance. For her, I hope that she is always able to accept those with whom she does not always agree."

Laney laughed and grabbed Gunner's beard. He laughed too and handled it like a champ when she yanked. I was helping disengage her little fist from his facial hair when we heard a horn honk around the front of the house.

"That's the clown's ride," I said. "Good thing that's over."

"Yes, good thing," Dad said.

He and my mother stepped forward. "Your father and I give Laney the gift of comfort and mercy. We hope that she will always be able to find them for herself and that she can bestow solace and compassion on those around her."

Lilith was next, and she looked more than eager. "I give her the ability to see the dark. Not only to be able to see in it but to also see it in others."

"I give her the unquenchable thirst for knowledge," Amelda said. "And the other Aunties will bring her gifts at another time. We don't want to interrupt the party, and there are some kids who look like they need something fun to do."

And something fun they got. When we saw the fae approaching the yard from the tree line behind the house, my family swooped in to take care of all the kids.

"Now, if all the moms would join me in the kitchen for a glass of wine, I would most appreciate it," my mother said.

Not one mom argued. They all filed into the house just as the fae came into the yard.

They were beautiful and nearly angelic, but instead of radiating white light, one of them glowed pink and the other was surrounded by a purple sparkling aura.

As if drawn by my daughter, they glided across the yard and stood before Gunner. Their shimmering gowns rustled in a soft wind that seemed to accompany them. It carried the scent of spring lilacs and a touch of sugar.

"We hope you don't mind," the one in pink said. "We wanted to give the little one a gift."

"I don't mind," I said. "What is the gift?"

"We give the only ones we can," the one in purple said. "I give her the gift of beauty both inside and out."

"And I give her song," said the one in pink. "Both the gift of melody and of a song in her heart even in the hardest of times."

Laney laughed again and reached for the fae. They smiled and each took one of her little hands while Gunner held her tight.

The fairies closed their eyes for a second, and when they opened them, the pink one said, "It is done."

"Thank you for allowing us to visit with you," the purple one added.

And then they left. The two fairies disappeared into the trees just as the moms came back out to the party with glasses of red or white wine in their hands.

After that, we opened some presents, ate cake, and the kids began to get tired. Laney needed a nap for sure, and the other mothers thanked us for the invitation before heading out to let their own little ones get some rest.

I was standing in a circle with Mom, Lilith, and one of the witch moms whose kid was like the Energizer Bunny when Thorn got a call from Jeremy.

He was working that day so Thorn could have it off, but he and Reggie were supposed to come over that night for a smaller party with Laney, me, and Thorn. Reggie had planned on coming to the party during the day if she could make it, but she'd been feeling under the weather.

While Thorn was off to the side of the yard talking to Jeremy on the phone and looking concerned, Dorian walked into the backyard. "I'm so sorry I'm late," he said and looked around. "Looks like I missed all of the festivities."

"But we're always happy to have you," I said. "Where's Isaac?"

"He's at the Brew Station. Apparently, that place has eaten two of our people today," Dorian said.

It was true. Vivian had wanted to come to Laney's party as well, but three of her people had called off with the flu. Apparently, it had been so bad that she'd had to call Isaac in on his day off to help her. I didn't mind, though. It was a kid's birthday party. The prospect had to be less than thrilling for all of my adult, and childless, friends.

"You didn't have to come," I said.

"Nonsense," Dorian said with a wave of his hand. "Besides, it looks like I missed all of the kid stuff anyway. Are you sure this wasn't a regular party and you told me it was a kiddie party to keep me away?"

I laughed. "No, it's just that little ones get tired. Most of them are gone. Mom's taking Laney inside for a nap too."

"What's your husband doing?" Dorian asked.

At that point, he was whisper-yelling into the phone and gesturing wildly with his free hand. "Fine, okay. I'll be there in five. You're explaining this to my wife," he said and hung up.

"That doesn't sound good," Dorian said.

"No, it doesn't," I replied.

We didn't say anything else for the few seconds it took Thorn to walk our way. He took a deep breath and rubbed the back of his neck nervously before speaking.

"I have to go," he said.

"I thought Jeremy had everything under control today," I shot back.

"He did, but there's been a murder," Thorn said. "I need to be there."

"Oh," I was my replay. "That's... It's been a while. I thought that maybe..."

"Yeah, that's what I thought too," Thorn said. "But we've had another, and I need to go to the scene."

"Where is the scene?" I asked instinctively.

"Kinsley," Thorn's voice warned.

"I'm not saying I'm going to go there. I'm just curious."

Thorn's eyes darted back and forth between me and Dorian. "I suppose the two of you are going to find out eventually anyway. There's no keeping anything quiet in this town."

"You're right about that," Dorian said.

"Fine," Thorn said and pinched the bridge of his nose. "I'll tell you but only because I know you're not going to leave your daughter on her first birthday to chase a killer. He was found on the playground over in Oak Park."

"The playground?" Dorian asked. "Were any kids around?"

"No, the playground was closed for them to put down fresh rubber mulch. Apparently, this happened between the time the work crew left, and anyone realized that the playground was open again."

"But kids saw the body?" I asked and swallowed a lump in my throat.

"No. Fortunately, it was a jogger who found the body. There was a family on their way to the playground, but the father got out of the car ahead of the mom and the kid. He kept them away."

Chapter Two

Thorn

I didn't want to leave Laney's birthday party. Even when I'd mentioned going inside while Chuckles the Clown did his act, I hadn't really meant it. It was true that I wasn't big on clowns, but for my daughter and my wife, I would have cowboyed up.

The story of why I hated clowns is... we'll just say it was interesting. It was a normal day at school. We lived in a small town, so most of the modern protocols regarding school security had, so far, passed us over.

Sure, there were metal detectors in high schools, but the elementary school was an open book. There wasn't a guard at the doors checking people in or out. No fence surrounded the outdoor playground area. Anybody could walk onto the school grounds and even into the building.

And one day, someone did.

I would learn later, as an adult, that a few counties over and across the state line, some of the schools had been on lockdown because of clown threats.

What's a clown threat? Apparently, someone had been posting on message boards about sneaking into schools and abducting children. At one school, again over the state line, a secretary received a cryptic letter made of cut-out magazine letters, construction paper, and red ink also threatening to abduct and kill children.

Given the nature of the letter, and creepy art project form it took, people assumed it was kids playing a prank. What else could it possibly be?

It was too much like something out of a cheesy horror movie to be real. Sure, they kept that school on a soft lockdown for a few days as a precaution, but the story never even made national news. The school board and local law enforcement kept it all under the radar. My father helped keep it all swept under the rug.

Trying to avoid a panic, they said...

Apparently, nobody in my school heard anything about it. Or if they did, they thought it was something that happened in that other state. Something that happened in the big city. (Not that any of the surrounding towns were actually big cities, but they were sprawling metropolises compared to the Podunk where I grew up.) People in my little town saw the state next door as being full of hippie liberals.

Folks believed that our town was still full of hard-working, God-fearing, gun-toting patriots. So, we were supposedly safe from the crime and debauchery of those dirty hippies. Something like that. I was a kid, so I only ever heard snippets of old men telling tales to my father. A man who by that point was far removed from who he'd been when he was sheriff in Coventry. Time and space away from Brighton had not served him well. But that's a digression…

The stories of apartment complexes in the city having to send out warning letters about clowns trying to lure kids into the woods didn't register with my neighbors. We were good country folk.

Stuff like that didn't happen in OUR town...

You get the drift.

But on that day, things did happen. I suppose anyone who saw the clown walking across the field toward the building probably thought he was there as part of an assembly or classroom party. Maybe the kids of Brooks Elementary School had earned a special treat.

From a distance, he would have looked like a regular clown dressed in a bright orange costume with almost elf-like red shoes. Later in life, I looked at photos of the clown after his arrest, and it struck me that his outfit looked like a prison jumpsuit. He looked like an escaped murderer who'd found some elf shoes from a Christmas costume. Strange how he was arrested in the same costume as I'd seen him in that day. He must have worn it all of the time.

Most clowns I remembered from before this incident wore bright rainbow wigs, but the man that day just had his face and bald head painted white. Black diamond makeup over his eyes gave him a menacing look as did the streaks of red down his forehead and cheeks.

I still don't know if those were makeup or blood. In my child's mind, it as makeup. A kid's brain will do anything to protect them from the horrible truths of the world, so I'll never know. I could've asked my father before he passed away, but I didn't.

Perhaps I hadn't wanted the truth.

The clown, John David Marlin, walked into my school that way with a fake smile and a handful of colorful balloons. By the time he crossed paths with me, he was down to one. I remember being disappointed because all he had left was a pink balloon. A rootin'-shootin' cowboy like me wanted nothing to do with a pink balloon. It was even worse when Sadie Clements walked past us with a red balloon. Why didn't she take pink? Girls, at the time, were gross and mean, and Sadie was the worst.

They found that red balloon in the woods outside the school. It was popped and half buried under dirt and leaves. They never found Sadie, though.

For most of my childhood, I reasoned and beat myself up over that moment. I refused his pink balloon because it was for girls, and was that why he took Sadie instead of me? If I had just taken the stupid balloon, would John David Marlin have plucked me off the playground at recess in her place? In my little boy mind, that would have been better. I could have fought him off. I would have karate chopped him in the throat and saved the day.

But he took Sadie. After that, they put a fence up around the playground and baseball diamond. After that, someone would ask adults what their business was if they were seen walking around the school. The secretary started a sign-in and sign-out sheet. You couldn't just walk in anymore. Gone was the illusion that no one would come to a school to harm children.

I realized for the first time that the world wasn't safe. It was a gut-wrenching, heart-shattering awakening. One that my father wasn't able to comfort me from because he was devastated too. He had failed as sheriff. The warning signs were all there, and he'd ignored them to keep the peace. Because it had been easier for him to stay silent rather than challenge people's notions of our town.

My mother wasn't around at the time either. She hadn't left us completely yet, but it was during the time when she'd drift in and out of our lives. When Sadie disappeared, it was one of the times she'd drifted off.

So, the incident burned a little hole in me. It was a wound that never healed.

One that for the most part didn't affect my daily life. But as I drove toward the crime scene to meet with Jeremy, I had to take a few deep breaths to steady my nerves. I could feel that little hole aching and itching deep down inside of me.

Part of me wondered if I'd find John David Marlin dead in the park. Was it possible that the entire thing had come full circle? Not likely. He'd be an elderly man if he were still around. He should have still been in prison, but that was a different story.

One that I could not get into without getting furious at the injustice of the world.

Instead, I assumed it was Chuckles from the party. How he'd gone from being drunk off cheap beer at my child's birthday party to dead in a public park in such a short time was a mystery I wasn't looking forward to solving.

And one I wouldn't have to…

As soon as I pulled up to Jeremy's cruiser, I could see that the man lying in the middle of the park with a large knife sticking out of him wasn't Chuckles.

"Another clown?" I puzzled as I got out of the cruiser. Jeremy stood outside the perimeter he'd created with police tape. Off to the side stood two men, but they weren't together.

"I'm sorry to have to call you away," Jeremy said as I approached. "I really didn't want to do it, but…"

"No, you did the right thing," I said. "I should be here for this, and Laney was getting ready to lie down for a nap anyway. The party was pretty much over."

"Are we still getting together this evening?" Jeremy asked.

"Unless this takes all night," I said, "which I sincerely hope it doesn't. What do we have?"

"Death by stabbing," Jeremy said.

"The killer was kind enough to leave us the weapon," I said.

"Very kind," Jeremy replied. "Very kind indeed, but what do you want to bet there are no prints?"

"I'm not taking that bet. Unless they want to be caught, there's no way we're getting fingerprints off that knife. The killer left it behind to send a message," I said. "That would be my guess anyway."

"What do you think the message is?" Jeremy asked. "First impressions."

"The clown did something to a kid," I said off the top of my head. "Someone killed him to avenge a loved one."

"That was fast," Jeremy said.

"Never did trust clowns," I said. "It's also possible the killer is a kid that the clown hurt. Maybe they are all grown up and out for vengeance. Who is it? Who's the victim?"

"Do you want to get closer and have a look?" Jeremy asked.

"Nah, let's let forensics do their thing. Until then, we can talk here," I said.

"They're not going to get much in a public park. Not much they can use anyway. There's probably tons of DNA and trace evidence here. And by evidence, I mean stuff that has nothing to do with this murder," Jeremy said.

"That's true, but all the same, I want to give them time at the scene. Any idea when they'll be here?" I asked.

"I called them as soon as dispatch got the call about a clown with a knife sticking out of him in the park. They should be here in a few minutes," Jeremy confirmed. "Victim's name is Dewey Prescott. His wallet was next to him on the ground. All of his money and credit cards were still inside. So, not a robbery."

"And who are these guys?" I asked and pointed to the two men a few yards away from us with their backs turned to the scene. "Looky-loos?"

"Nope, these are our initial witnesses," Jeremy said. "The guy in the gray muscle tank and running shorts is our jogger who discovered the body. Name's Jason Keyes. The guy in jeans and a Slayer t-shirt is Richard Mayer. He's the one who was bringing his wife and kid to the park. We sent the wife and kid home since he stopped them before they saw anything. I didn't want to chance the kid seeing this. I hope that's all right."

"It was the right thing to do," I confirmed. "We can always go talk to them at the house if we need to. Have you interviewed either of them yet?"

"I talked to the dad and took his statement. He just walked up, saw the body, and then went back to his car. I told him to hang around in case you wanted to speak with him."

"All right, I'll go see if he remembers anything else, and then I'll talk to the jogger. Looks like there are some people headed this way with their phones out. Can you run interference?"

"Will do, sir," Jeremy said.

He took off in the direction of the potential gawkers, and I made my way over to Richard Mayer. He had his hands shoved in his jeans pockets and was looking around in every direction but at the body.

"Hello," I said as I approached him and stuck out my hand for a shake. "I'm Sheriff Thorn Wilson."

"Richard Mayer," he said and shook my hand.

"I just wanted to follow up with you, and then you can be on your way. I understand you already spoke with my deputy."

"I have," he said. "I'm sorry that I can't be more help."

"I wanted to ask you if you'd thought of anything else while you were waiting?" I pushed on through.

"I haven't," he said.

"Nothing as you were parking the car or maybe you saw something strange as you were driving up to the park. Anything you can think of might help. Even if it seems insignificant to you," I said. "You just never know."

"Your deputy said the same thing," Richard answered. "I really didn't see anything at all. I saw the man over there jog past and stop. He turned around and went back, and I watched him for a moment as my wife got our kid out of the car. I saw the body on the ground, and it didn't register at first. So, I started walking that way to see what the guy was looking at. When I saw it, I told my wife to get back in the car."

"Did anyone else approach the scene before my deputy got here?" I asked.

"No, we all knew the playground was closed for the day. But I went and got burgers for lunch and saw them leaving on the way back. The kid's been pretty riled up today, so I figured a trip to the park was in order," Richard said.

"Okay, well, if you think of anything else, give my office a call. Even if it's just that you remember seeing someone walking down the street. All right?" I asked.

"Will do, sir," Richard said.

As he walked away, I approached Jason Keyes, the jogger. He was in his late thirties or perhaps early forties. Well-built and tan. So, I figured he spent a lot of time outdoors. I wanted to ask him about that, and about how much time he spent in the park.

"Hello, Mr. Keyes. I'm Sheriff Thorn Wilson," I said and extended my hand. He took it and offered a half-hearted shake. "Thank you for your patience today. I know this isn't a pleasant situation, and I'm going to get you out of here as soon as I can."

"I think my run is ruined now," he returned.

That seemed like a strange response, but everyone handled things differently. Some people couldn't stop thinking about the traumatic thing they'd witnessed, and others had to shut it off, so they didn't go crazy.

"Can you tell me about that?" I asked. "As much as you can remember."

"I run every afternoon after work. I work at home, so I get up at five and start for the day. That usually means I'm done around lunchtime. I eat and then run, but today I had to wait. The rest of my path was fine, but I don't like to deviate from my route. It's important to establish a habit and stick to it. Running through the park helps me do that," Jason said. "So, I waited until the park would be open when I got this far. They posted the closure schedule last week. I saw it on the board."

"Okay, so do you remember seeing anything out of the ordinary during your run?" I asked.

"You mean aside from having to delay it while they worked on the playground?"

Jason asked. "I still don't understand why they had to close the entire park just to put mulch on the playground."

"I think that's just for everyone's safety," I answered. "Did you see anybody out of the ordinary before you came upon the body? Did you see anyone acting strange?"

"There was nobody around," Jason answered quickly. Almost too quickly. "That safety thing really worked out well..." he trailed off.

"Is there something else?" I prodded.

He let out a big sigh. "I don't know if it was anything."

"You should let me decide that. Tell me what you saw. You never know what might help," I said.

"Well, you know there's a wooded area over there off the park, right? It connects to a neighborhood on the other side, but there's a pretty good number of trees. I like to run through that neighborhood and the little trail through the trees. While I was running through, I thought I saw something a few hundred feet off in the distance. Off in that direction, I think," Jason said and pointed at an area of trees near the edge of the playground. "Anyway, it looked like a person dressed in bright colors. They were very pale, but I could have sworn they had this insanely bright red hair."

"Like a clown?" I asked.

"It's weird, right. Because the guy is already dead. If I wasn't such a rational person, I could have sworn I was seeing a ghost," Jason said.

"So, the person you saw looked just like the deceased?" I asked.

"No," Jason said and shook his head. "I guess they didn't. The dead clown is wearing a rainbow wig, and the one I saw in the woods had red hair. And I think a red nose. I don't know, because he was there and then gone. I would swear that it was just my imagination getting the better of me, but I hadn't found the dead guy yet. So, what would have put the idea of clowns into my head?"

"Your statement is that you saw a clown in the woods, but only for a moment. They were in costume so you couldn't identify who it was?" I asked.

"Yeah, and I'm not sure that's the strangest part," Jason said and trailed off again.

"What is?" I asked.

"I thought I saw something shiny in his hand. Thinking back, it's almost as if he flashed it at me before he was gone," Jason said and then rubbed the back of his neck nervously. "It looked like he was holding a machete."

"A machete?" I asked.

"Yeah, like a killer clown in the woods with a machete," Jason said. "I know how it sounds, but it's what I remember."

"Anything else?" I asked. "Anything at all?"

"I thought I might have seen him again. While we were waiting for you guys to get here. I called for that other guy to look, but by the time he turned around, the clown was gone again. I'm sure he thinks I'm completely nuts," Jason said. "I'm starting to think I'm completely nuts. I'm not ordering lunch from that deli again. All that sodium might be affecting my brain."

"He didn't mention it to me," I replied and ignored his comment about lunch. "But if you think of anything else, please call us at the station. Anything at all might help."

"Can I finish my run now?" Jason asked, but then he looked at the watch on his wrist. Something I wasn't used to seeing very often. Not many people wore watches anymore. "Crap, never mind. I've got a video call with an international client in fifteen minutes. I really do need to go."

"That's fine," I said and stepped out of his way. "Just remember to call us if you think of anything."

Jason waved me off and took off jogging toward what I presumed was home. Hopefully, Jeremy had gotten all of the preliminary report information like his address, but it wouldn't matter too much. People in Coventry weren't hard to track down.

I sat in my cruiser after the crime scene team and then the coroner arrived. The clown on the playground was dead, but I still didn't want to be near him. I actually felt better with the car between us and my doors locked.

My eyes kept darting over to the forest as I expected to get a glimpse of the machete-wielding clown Jason had seen. The situation had to be just about my worst nightmare. The only thing worse than the possibility of clown-on-clown violence breaking out in Coventry would have been if my wife or daughter was sick. But how was I supposed to deal with a machete-wielding clown stalking Coventry? The rumor would spread fast, and so would the hysteria.

Chapter Three

Kinsley

My friends were all at the house in time for dinner. Well, everybody but Jeremy and Thorn. We tried waiting for them to eat, but by the third time I was about to get a piece of the birthday cake, I decided we needed a real meal. My stomach felt ready to consume itself. I hated it when I got that hungry.

We'd considered ordering take-out, but the girls and I ended up cooking. Viv and Reggie helped me in the kitchen while Isaac and Dorian tried their hands at watching Laney.

My parents had gone home as my friends began to arrive but told me to call them if I needed someone to babysit. I told them I wasn't going to have them take Laney on her birthday, but they said she wouldn't know the difference and the offer was open if I changed my mind.

Much to Dorian's surprise, and Isaac's delight, Dorian was really good with Laney. I got the vibe off the couple that Isaac wanted a baby and he was doing his best to convince Dorian it was a good idea. If they wanted a family, they deserved it after everything they'd been through.

Laney seemed to be doing the heavy lifting when it came to persuading Dorian, though. When I'd pop out of the kitchen to check on them, Dorian would be grinning from ear to ear. Isaac would try to get a chance to play with Laney, and Dorian was hogging her. I even thought perhaps she liked him better than Uncle Gunner, and she'd been completely smitten with Coventry's former sheriff.

By the time the girls and I had dinner on the table, Thorn and Jeremy were coming through the front door. It seemed like he always had impeccable timing when it came to eating dinner.

"Wow, that smells amazing," Jeremy said.

"Since there were three of us in the kitchen, we thought we'd try something a little more complicated," Reggie called back.

I took the tray of empanadas to the dining room table. I figured since there were so many of us, we'd actually use the dining room instead of crowding around the kitchen table.

We'd made three kinds of empanadas including fiesta chicken, goat cheese and spinach, and Jamaican jerk with ground beef. That one was my favorite. I'd had them numerous times from a bakery that sold its wares at a farmer's market, but I'd never attempted to make them myself. I thought the girls and I had outdone ourselves.

We'd also made side dishes of refried black beans and Spanish rice. It was kind of a hodgepodge meal, but Jeremy was right, every dish smelled incredible. My stomach growled, and it took all of my willpower not to grab an empanada and snarf it down.

"Okay, guys, time to eat," I said. "Dorian or Isaac, why don't you bring Laney in here? I'll put her in the highchair."

I had a plate fixed for her too. I knew she would love the beans and rice, but I'd also cut half a goat cheese and spinach empanada into bite-sized pieces.

Dorian and Isaac brought Laney into the dining room. Dorian handed Laney over to Isaac, and Isaac put her in the highchair. Laney looked down at the food in front of her on the tray and clapped her little hands with delight.

She started to dig in right away. I almost had to stop her from putting fistfuls of the cheesy empanada, rice, and beans into her mouth. Fortunately, Isaac sat down right next to her, and distracted her from eating as quickly.

Thorn and Jeremy joined us in the dining room while everyone took their chosen seats and got ready to dig in. Thorn was just about to spoon some of the black beans onto his plate when his phone rang. He almost ignored it, but I could see the

47

look on his face. He was devoted to his job, and he could not ignore the ringing phone.

He stood up again and took the call in the living room. I wanted to follow him out and listen to what was going on, but I had a dining room full of guests who were ready to eat. Plus, I was starving, and it really wasn't any of my business. As much as my curiosity wanted it to be, I needed to let Thorn do his work. My job that evening was to have a good time with my friends and Laney.

Thorn came back into the dining room a few minutes later with grim expression set on his face. "I have to go," he said. "Something's happened, and I need to get over to the park right away."

"I should come with you, boss," Jeremy said as he started to push away from the table and stand up.

"No, it's fine. Enjoy your dinner. I'll be back in a few minutes."

"Well, what's happened?" I asked. "You can't just say something like that and take off."

"Can I speak with you in the other room?" Thorn asked. "Just a quick second."

I followed thorn into the other room. I could hear everyone in the dining room quietly trying to get up and follow us as well, but the chairs squeaking across the wooden floor made too much noise for them to be stealthy. So, they had to sit there and listen from the other room. I could swear I heard Dorian groan in defeat. The reporter in him must have been going nuts.

When we got into the living room, Thorn eyed the front door. "I think maybe we should step out there," he said.

"Why? Because everyone is listening?" I asked.

"Exactly," Thorn responded.

I followed Thorn outside to the front porch and closed the door quietly behind us. It was a beautiful night. There were crickets chirping off in the distance, and I could hear frogs as well. The air smelled of flowers and a gentle breeze cooled my skin. "We probably should have eaten outside," I said. "It's a nice night for it."

Thorn turned to me and we stood on the front porch facing each other. "You guys can move the festivities outside. You've got enough hands to make it light work, but I can't help. Some kids called in a clown sighting at the same park where the murder occurred earlier," Thorn said.

"What are you talking about?" I asked. "Did you say clowns?"

"I'm sorry I didn't get the chance to tell you about what happened today. A clown was murdered in the park and the man who found the dead clown said that he saw another one off in the woods. That clown had a machete. According to the witness anyway," Thorn stated.

"Oh, geez," I said and rubbed my palms against my eyes like I could ground out the bad mental image Thorn's words had produced in my mind's eye. "You're saying that there is a dead clown and another killer clown loose in Coventry?" I asked.

"Yes, that appears to be about the sum of what's going on," Thorn said. "I'm not really sure what it's all about, but I'm going to figure it out. Right now, though, some kids have called in a clown sighting, and I need to go sort that out."

"Okay," I said. "I'll stay here and hold down the fort. What do you want me to tell everybody? Because, you know as well as I do that they're going to have questions after you dragged me out onto the porch to discuss this."

Thorn rubbed his jaw thoughtfully. His hand moved to the back of his neck where he appeared to be trying to soothe away some tension. He let out an exasperated breath and then his face relaxed. He offered me a soft, reassuring smile. "Just tell them the truth," he said. "There is no point in trying to hide any of this. It's all going to be spread around Coventry soon enough."

I went back into the house and proceeded to tell everyone the story that Thorn had just told me. Of course, all my friends had tons of questions. Dorian, in particular, pleaded with Jeremy to fill him in on the details of the murder, but Jeremy was the only person who was more of a stickler for his job than Thorn.

So, the evening had to proceed with just us having dinner and normal conversation. It was difficult not to pester Jeremy with questions, but I didn't want to be rude. He'd already said he wasn't going to give details of the case, so it was pointless to press the issue. At one point, though, Jeremy could tell that I was uneasy. I ate, but my stomach started to feel unsettled. It must have shown on my face.

"It's okay, Kinsley," Jeremy said. "You know that it was probably just some teenagers messing around. Most likely, they heard the rumors about the clowns, and some dumb kids decided that they wanted to get in on the action. They probably thought it was fun and spooky because they don't know any better."

"I can see that," I said. "But it still bothers me. Plus, I know Thorn has to be uncomfortable. You know that he hates clowns, right?"

"He didn't say anything," Jeremy said. "But I could tell that he looked uncomfortable at the scene. I just thought it was because it was a dead clown with a knife sticking out of his back."

"Did you really have to tell me those details?" I asked with an uneasy chuckle. "I don't know that I really needed that particular visual. Can you tell me something?"

"That depends," Jeremy said. "Are you going to ask me details about the case?"

"Just one detail," I said. "You know we had a clown here earlier for Laney's birthday, right? Was that the clown died?"

"It wasn't," Jeremy said. "It was a completely different clown."

"You're joking, right?" I asked. "So, you're saying that there was a different clown killed in town today? And there's an entire other clown that's menacing people in the woods by one of the playgrounds?"

"I know it all sounds very bizarre," Jeremy said. "Thorn and I haven't really had time to discuss it much yet. We wanted to get here as soon as we could to have dinner and then sleep on it. I figured we could have a meeting in the morning to discuss the issue further."

"But he didn't think that there would be another clown sighting tonight?" I asked.

"How could he?" Jeremy asked. "The clown the witness thought he saw this morning…we don't even know if that was real. He just thought he saw it."

"I'd say it's pretty real now," I countered.

A couple of hours later, I began to get even more nervous. Thorn hadn't returned home, and he wasn't answering his phone either.

When Jeremy stepped outside to take a call, it felt like someone punched me in the stomach. The look in his eyes sent a shiver down my spine. I nearly followed him out, but Reggie grabbed my hand.

She and Jeremy were the only ones who hadn't gone home yet. They'd decided to stay with me and wait until we heard from Thorn.

"He said he'd be right back," I practically whispered.

"I know," Reggie said and squeezed my hand.

I stood there in the living room watching the front door. I was willing it to open and for Jeremy to come back inside and say that Thorn had a flat tire on the cruiser, or he'd gotten called away to deal with a drunk driver. It had to be something like that. But the look on Jeremy's face when he came back inside told me that something was definitely wrong. My stomach clenched like I was going to be sick.

"What is it?" I asked. "Please tell me. You're scaring me right now."

Jeremy took a deep breath. "He's in the emergency room, Kinsley. There was an attack."

Only, it felt like the room was spinning around me, and the floor was going to rise up and smack me in the face. I slumped and felt myself fall against Reggie. To her credit, she caught me and didn't let me fall to the floor.

"I'll take her," Reggie said. "I'll take her to the hospital to see him."

"Okay," Jeremy replied. "I'll take the baby over to her parents' house."

"No," I countered. "We're taking Laney with us." I felt some of my strength coming back then. I felt my back straighten, and I knew that I had to be strong for my husband.

"Are you sure?" Reggie asked. "We can take the baby over to your parents' house. It would probably be easier for everybody if she wasn't there. At least until we know what's going on with Thorn. Until we know… how bad it is."

I thought about it for a few moments. She was right. It would be easier if we didn't take the baby to the hospital right away. As much as I wanted Laney with me, I had to do what was best for everyone.

"Okay," I relented. "You can take Laney to my parents' place, but could you please tell them to meet us at the hospital soon? I want to have Laney with me as soon as we know what's going on. I hate to do this on her birthday."

"All right," Jeremy said. "I'll tell them to meet you at the hospital after you call them."

I helped Reggie and Jeremy get Laney changed and we put her car seat in Jeremy's car.

"Don't you need to be there to make a report?" I asked Jeremy. Suddenly it had occurred to me that he might have official business involving the attack.

"They're still working on him, Kinsley. I'll be there in fifteen minutes, okay? I want to take your daughter to her grandparents' house. I want to make sure that Thorn's little girl is safe and cared for. It's what he'd want. Besides, every other deputy is already there. Let me do this for you guys."

That made sense. "Thank you," I said.

I waved at them as they backed out of the driveway, but Laney had already drifted off. Something about being in a car knocks a baby completely out.

"Let's go," Reggie said. "Are you ready? We should get going."

I could tell that Reggie was nervous and rattled by the experience. That only made me more nervous.

Chapter Four

The first thing that struck me when I walked through the automatic doors of the emergency room was the smell. It was that antiseptic scent that's like nothing else you've ever experienced. It doesn't smell like any kind of cleaner you can get at the grocery store and doesn't even smell like the stuff that they use in office buildings or schools.

The second thing I noticed was how chilly it was. I was in the emergency room, but I couldn't help thinking that the people who were there waiting to be seen by a doctor had to be cold. The combination of the strange, antiseptic smell and chilly air was enough to turn my stomach and send a shiver down my spine.

I walked up to a central desk and stood at a long white counter waiting for a nurse to have time to speak to me. I ended up waiting a couple of minutes because the emergency room was hopping that night. Although I could have kept myself busy listening to the din of conversations going on around me, I couldn't focus on anything but my worry for Thorn.

In the back of my mind, I wondered if I would be able to heal him. It was true that Meri had returned all of our magical powers, but was I a strong enough to help my husband? All I knew was that I needed to get to him as soon as possible. So, I nearly jumped out of my skin when a nurse finally appeared before me and asked, "How can I help you, honey?"

I told her that I was there to see my husband, Sheriff Thorn Wilson. I said that he had been brought in after some sort of accident or attack on the job. The nurse's face grew grave, she put her head down and came around the counter to stand next to me.

"Right this way, sweetie," she said. "The doctors said to keep the family in the waiting room until they had a chance to look him over, but there's no way I'm going to keep you away from him. It's just not what we do here."

She said it is not what we do here, and I
knew she was talking about nurses. The
doctors may have wanted to keep me
away, but this was a nurse. She knew that
what he needed and what I needed was
for us to be together. Maybe she even
knew I could heal him. I was too focused
on Thorn to read her for possible witchcraft
or traces of other supernatural powers.

"Will you get in trouble?" I asked. "I don't
want you to get in trouble for letting me
back." Even as I said the words, I knew I
was still going to go back. Nothing could
keep me from Thorn, but I felt the need to
at least put up a perfunctory performance.

"I don't care what that old bat says," the
nurse replied. "They can't run this ship
without us, so what I say goes around
here."

"The head nurse?" I asked.

"That I am," she replied. "My name is
Becky, and if you need anything. I'm who
you should ask. But I should warn you,
head nurse shifts are always a little crazy in
the emergency room, sometimes I'm a tad

busy. I'll do my best if you need anything, though."

Part of me knew the red carpet treatment was because Thorn was Coventry's sheriff. The kinship between the ER staff and first responders meant he'd be a priority. Thorn wouldn't have liked that, but it wouldn't matter. He was about to have a miraculous recovery.

I wasn't prepared to see Thorn, and the sight of his injuries took my breath away.

Becky squeezed my hand. "He'll be all right," she said. "Let me know if y'all need anything."

As soon as she was gone from the room, I rushed to Thorn's side. He was covered in bruises that were just beginning to turn swollen and angry. He'd also apparently suffered from several cuts or stabs. I took his hand and placed my other over his heart.

I began to heal him, but for the first time, I could feel my life force draining into him. I couldn't just heal him. I had to give myself to do it.

Still, I pressed on. As I began to feel weak, Thorn's eyes fluttered open. "No," he said and squeezed my hand. "Don't do it."

"I have to," I replied. "I can't just leave you like this."

"It's hurting you," Thorn said. "I can feel it. You have to stop."

"No," he said, and before I could protest further, Jeremy walked into the room. He was followed by a doctor.

The doctor eyed me right away and gave an almost imperceptible shake of his head. He did not approve of me being in the room, but he kept his feelings to himself.

"Someone will be here to take you for your scans, and once that's done, we'll get you up to surgery," the doctor said.

"Surgery!" I yelped.

"Is this your wife?" the doctor asked.

"I am," I said before Thorn could speak. "What is the surgery for?"

"Why don't you head over to the registrar's office?" the doctor said. "There's some paperwork that still needs to be taken care of before the surgery. The sooner you get that done, the better."

"Is it really necessary?" Thorn asked. "I'd really like for her to be here."

"I'm afraid it is," the doctor replied. "Shouldn't take long. The process is straightforward and all computerized now, so she'll be back in a jiffy. I'll make sure they don't take you away for surgery until she gets here, and all the time while she's gone, you'll be getting your scans anyway. She can't go along for that."

"Okay," Thorn relented. "Honey, do you mind? I need to discuss some of what happened with Jeremy anyway, and I can't have anyone else around when we do that. Plus, the crime scene techs still need to do some… processing. Particulars of the case and all."

I didn't know if he really meant he wasn't going to tell me what had happened, or if he was just putting on a show for the doctor. I also wondered what they were going to process? Him? What I did know was that there was a burning desire deep inside my gut to find out what happened to Thorn and who had done it. Because that person was going to pay.

"I'll go," I said. "But only because I want to make this process as easy as possible for you. Jeremy, will you call me when my parents get to the hospital with Laney? On second thought, could you call them and tell them to come here? I want them to be here while Thorn is in surgery."

"Of course," Jeremy said. "I'll call them now. Tell them to meet you here in fifteen to twenty minutes? Okay?"

"Thank you," I replied. "That should give me time to get the paperwork done."

I left the room after that, and left Thorn, Jeremy, and the doctor to discuss things. It really felt like I was being treated like a little baby who couldn't handle things, but I knew Thorn didn't mean to make it that way. Someone would tell me what was going on soon, I just knew it.

The thing was, I had no idea where the registrar's office was. I looked around for signs that would point me in the right direction, and I found nothing. I searched for some sort of kiosk that would give directions to the different departments in the hospital, but I didn't want to go too far from the emergency room.

So, I trudged back up to the emergency room desk, and I stood there waiting quietly for Becky to get done talking to another nurse. She was halfway over to me when the ambulance bay doors opened up. Two paramedics wheeled a gurney in quickly. "Stab wound," one of them said. "Collapsed lung." After that he rattled off a bunch of vital statistics, and I stood there looking in horror, unable to peel my eyes from the man who lay on the gurney. It had to have been more than one stab wound. It looked like he was covered in them. But the thing that had me stock-still in abject horror was the red balloon tied around his wrist.

Fortunately, a janitor pushed his cart down the hallway just as I realized I still needed to find the registrar's office. "Excuse me, sir, I need to find the registrar's office. Can you help me?"

Must have been something in my eyes because the man's grizzled expression softened. "I'll show you," he said. "I know every inch of this building."

"Thank you so much," I said.

I really was in and out of the registrar's office in under ten minutes. I made my way back to Thorn's room, and when I walked in, he was sitting up messing with the remote to fix the TV channel. I pulled a chair next to his bed and sat down next to him. After taking his hand, I considered trying to heal him again. But, Thorn immediately picked up on what I wanted to do, and he shook his head no.

"Don't do it, sweetie," Thorn said.

"I just don't understand," I said. "I don't understand why I can't just heal you. I need to heal you. I don't want you to have to have surgery or stay in the hospital."

"Well, if it's any consolation, I am feeling much better," Thorn said. "What healing you were able to do to do, it made all the difference in the world."

"I guess we'll just have to wait and see what the scans say," I said. "Have you had any of them? I know I wasn't gone for very long."

"No," Thorn said. "I haven't had any the tests, but they said they'll be here any minute to take me back."

Right on cue, two nurses came into the room. "We just need to borrow him for a few minutes," one of the nurses said. "We'll have them back in a jiffy. You can wait here or radiology has a waiting room."

I stayed out of the way while they got Thorn ready to go. "I'll stay here. I'm expecting my parents and our daughter soon."

After they wheeled Thorn out for his various scans, my mom and dad showed up with Laney. She'd been sleeping in my mother's arms, but as soon as she saw me, she woke up and reached for me to take her.

"Hi, sweetie," I said and took her from my mom. "How are you, honey?"

She gave me a kiss and put her head on my shoulder in response.

"She's doing great," my dad said. "Are you sure you want us to have her here, though?"

"Remy, we talked about this," my mom said. "If she wants us all here, then we will be here."

"I know," my dad said sheepishly. "It just seems like it would be better if Laney stayed home with one of us. Or, if you need both of us here with you, you can take her over to Amelda's or Lilith's. You know, I bet even Viv or Reggie would watch her."

"I know," I admitted. "I just feel bad about leaving her with someone else on her birthday."

"Sweetie," my dad began, "you know she has no idea what's going on. She's not going to remember any of this."

"We don't know that for sure," I said. "What if she does retain memories from when she's young? It's not unheard of."

"It is possible," my mom admitted. "And I know everybody wants to believe that their baby is special, and she is, but not like that. Kinsley, she's not going remember any of this."

"Okay, well, can we just hang out for a little while and find out what's going on? If it turns out that Thorn has to go to surgery or has to spend the night, I will figure out something else to do with Laney."

Even as I said the words, though, I knew I didn't really mean them. I couldn't stand the thought of being separated from her while sitting in the hospital waiting for Thorn to get out of surgery. I just had to keep her quiet and happy, and everyone would see that it was fine for her to be there with us.

"Guys, I need to talk to you about something," I said.

"What is it, sweetie?" Dad asked.

"Well, when I got here, I tried to heal Thorn," I said. "And I was able to heal him, but something else happened. While I was healing him, it seemed like it was draining my life force. That's the best way I can think to describe it."

"What do you mean?" Mom asked.

"I'm not exactly sure," I said. "My life force was draining into him as I healed him. I was using the same magic that I always did but giving to him was taking from me. It was so obvious, even Thorn felt it. He told me to stop. Otherwise, we wouldn't be having this conversation. We'd be on our way home, but I couldn't heal him."

"I had wondered about that," Mom said. "I thought perhaps you just hadn't had enough time alone with him yet, but if you already tried...We thought that we got all of our magic back, but maybe things have changed. Just because Meri restored our powers doesn't mean that they were left unchanged."

"What if it's just me?" I asked. "What if there something wrong with me? You guys can try to heal him."

"No," Dad said. "I know what you're talking about. I didn't even think about it, but the same thing happened the other day when I tried to heal someone. Just an old buddy who cut his hand while we were working on his shed. I felt the same thing. I thought it was just because of the darkness that I've experienced before. But maybe it is all of us."

"But what could be changing things?" I asked. "That's what bothers me, and why just healing? The rest of my powers have been fine."

Mom walked across the room and put her hand on my shoulder. "It's okay, sweetie. At least you were able to heal him some, and he's going to be okay. You know that, right?"

"I do," I said. "He will be okay, but I didn't want him to have to have surgery."

"Just wait until the tests come back," dad said. "Maybe he won't."

I looked at my mom, and a strange look came over her face.

"What is it?" I asked. "Did you... Did you just see something? A premonition or a vision?"

"Is there something that you want to tell us?" Mom asked.

"No," I said and shook my head. "I have no idea what you're talking about. Did you see something? Is something going to happen?"

Mom laughed and patted my shoulder again. "Everything's just fine, sweetie. Something good is coming into our lives, but I don't think now is the time to talk about it. You've got enough on your plate but trust me when I say it's a good thing. There's plenty of time to discuss new arrivals once your husband is better."

"And that's it? You're not going to tell me anything?" I asked, but the way she smiled made me feel warm and fuzzy. There was genuine joy radiating from my mother's eyes. Whatever it was, I suddenly felt like everything was going to be all right.

"Like a said, sweetie, in due time. Just... make sure you're eating plenty of fruits and vegetables."

I was going to inquire further as to what kind of amazing surprise required me to eat more fruits and vegetables, but the nurses came back with Thorn. His arrival, plus Laney needing to eat, completely distracted me from the thought.

They'd brought Thorn back after about an hour. He looked really tired, but he didn't look near death the way he did when I first arrived.

At some point, while we were waiting for the doctor to come back with the scan results, Thorn and I finally got a few minutes alone. My mom and dad were out of the room with Laney walking around and probably getting some air.

She didn't particularly like being in the hospital, and it was evident I was going to have to let them take her somewhere else soon. I didn't know how long I had before she blew her top, but she could go at any time.

"You look pale," Thorn interrupted my thoughts. "You look like you're feeling worse than I do."

"I'm fine," I said. "Don't worry about me. You're the one we should be worried about."

"I'm okay," Thorn replied. "But seriously, Kinsley, you're pale and a little shaky. What is going on?"

"Well, I had a bit of a shock when I was out in the emergency room." I realized the adrenaline rush from finding out Thorn was in the hospital and then seeing that stabbing victim was wearing off. I felt wrung out, and if not for Thorn needing me, I'd have dove head-first into a plate of nachos and then my bed.

"So, it's not from healing me?" Thorn asked. "Because I'd hate to think that you made yourself sick trying to help me."

"Well, it's not that. I'm sure you get to hear about it soon enough. Maybe Jeremy or your other deputies are just waiting until they know for sure how you're doing. But, when I was out there looking for the registrar's office, they brought in another stabbing victim. He... He looked bad, Thorn."

"I'm sorry you had to see that," Thorn said. He put his hand over mine on the crisp white bedsheet and squeezed. "I should get a hold of Jeremy, though. If people are still getting killed, we'll need to do something about it. We need extra patrols, and we might have to call in the County to help with that. I just don't have enough people to increase patrols twenty-four hours per day."

"Yeah," I said. "This is bad. You being stuck in here in the hospital, and... Well... Thorn, he had a balloon tied around his wrist. It has to have been another clown. They must be trying to send some sort of message, but what is it?"

"No," Thorn said. "You are not getting involved in this."

"I already am," I replied. "I'm already involved, because you're in here after being attacked... Were you attacked by a clown?"

"I don't know. I went to go check things out because we had a report of another clown sighting but the sucker hit me over the head from behind. I was knocked out, and I didn't get a good look at who did it."

"Well," I said. "At least you were unconscious when he was... stabbing you. I'm sorry, I shouldn't be making you relive this."

"It's okay. I'm going to have to talk about it with just about everybody, so it didn't bother me to talk about it with you. Plus, thanks to you and whatever excellent painkillers they're giving me, I'm not really feeling any pain. I actually feel pretty good now," Thorn said. "It's like swimming in an ocean of warm, fuzzy blankets."

"That's good" I replied. "I do not want you to be in any pain."

Later, the doctor came into the room and told us that Thorn didn't need surgery. The doc looked surprised, happy, and confused all at once. He told us that Thorn had had some sort of scar tissue possibly from previously healed wounds that had protected his organs from major damage. Thorn and I knew that scar tissue was actually from me healing him, but the doctor didn't know. He didn't ever have to know.

So less than an hour later, the nurses showed up to help Thorn upstairs to his new room on the general floor. As it turned out, he didn't need surgery, but they were going to keep him overnight for observation. I thought that was mostly because the doctor was so confused, but I wasn't going to argue. We could handle having him in the hospital for one night. So, everybody trudged upstairs and once they put us in a private room, I helped get Thorn settled.

Unfortunately, Thorn had left his wallet down in the emergency room. "I'll get it," I said when a nurse offered to have someone bring it up. "It'll be faster if I just go."

"Thank you, sweetie," Thorn said. Unspoken between us was my knowledge that he wouldn't like having someone else handle his wallet.

My mom and dad were staying in the room with Thorn while I ran downstairs, and Laney was asleep on my dad's lap. I took the elevator back down to the first floor and the emergency room, and I found Becky within a couple of minutes.

"Do you have a moment?" she asked.

"Sure," I said. "What is it?"

"I'm about to go on break, will you join me? I'm not going to smoke or anything like that. I'd just like to have some privacy."

"Sure," I said. I followed her outside to the parking lot, and we stood next to one of the concrete structures holding up the parking lot lighting. I was a little confused, but I was also intrigued.

"I need your help with something," Becky said.

"Of course," I replied. "How can I help you?"

"I thought I recognized you. You're the woman that owns the shop down on the square, right? You own the place that sells the herbs and the crystals?"

"I do," I said. "Summoned Goods and Sundries."

"Yes, that's the place I'm thinking of," Becky said. "I was just wondering if… If you guys have anything for pain?"

"For pain?" I asked. "Like, what kind of pain?"

"The inexplicable kind," Becky said. "I've had this pain in my torso and back for months, and the doctors here can't tell me what is. I've had MRIs and CAT scans and ultrasounds, and nothing definitive has come up. I've had extensive bloodwork and that hasn't found anything definitive either. It's like mystery pain, but sometimes it feels like... Like I'm dying. I've even had a psych consult because I started to think it was just in my head."

"And did that help?" I asked.

"It helped with me feeling like I wanted to take my own life over this pain, but I don't believe it's in my head anymore. I'm starting to think that everybody else does," Becky said. "I just need help. Any kind of relief at all. Just simply take the edge off. I think I can get myself together better if I just hurt even a little less."

"And you don't want to take painkillers?" I asked, but I already knew the answer to that. If she wanted to go that route, Becky already would have done it. Instead, she was looking for something else.

"There have been a couple of doctors here who suggested it. They have tried to get me to start taking some pretty intense painkillers," Becky said. "They mean well, and at least they believe me. I know they do, but what happens when you start down that road? I've seen it in here just about every day. These people that once had normal lives, and they come in here looking for drugs because they are so addicted and desperate. Some of them even hurt themselves to get them. I don't want to end up like that. I've had family that ended up like that. I just need something... More natural? Does that make sense?"

"It does," I said. "I can understand not wanting to start on painkillers. You know, I'm sure that I can whip up something to help you. Would you be open to more than just herbs? I mean, I have herbs that will help you, Becky. I'll bring you something tomorrow, and I think you should I feel a lot better but I have some other things that might help you too. I just need to know if you're open to them?"

"Oh, honey, I'm open to anything at this point. You can bring me herbs, candles, crystals. Heck, you could bring me a cat, and I would accept it. You know what? Probably don't bring me a cat," she said with a laugh. "I work a lot of hours at this hospital. Poor thing would be alone all the time."

I couldn't help but laugh too. "I won't bring you a cat. I have a cat but couldn't part with him if you held a gun to my head. I do have some of those other things though. So along with the herbs, if you believe, I think things are going to get a lot better for you."

"Oh, my gosh," Becky said and pulled me into a tight hug. She felt like a python squeezing the life out of me, but I was still laughing. When she let me go, Becky said, "I'm working a double tomorrow, so whenever you get here, just give me a call and I'll come out and meet you as soon as I can." She slipped me a card with her phone number on it, and I tucked it into my purse.

"Are you going to be all right tonight?" I asked. "I feel bad leaving you in pain for another day. My husband's upstairs though…"

"Don't you worry about it," Becky said. "Just knowing that I'm going to be feeling better, it's lifting my spirits. I might take one of those pills the doctor prescribed, just to get me through the night. But I know that I won't have to take any more of them, so that should be fine, right?"

"Of course," I replied. "I hate to think of you in pain, but nobody's going to think badly of you if you need to take some medicine."

We parted ways and I watched Becky walk back into the emergency room with a pep in her step. She was even whistling by the time she got back to the nurses' station. I left her and went to the elevator to go back upstairs and take Thorn his wallet.

"It's getting late," Mom said as soon as I stepped into the room.

"You guys can go," I said. "it's beyond late, and I can handle Laney now. We'll be fine until they discharge Thorn in the morning."

"I meant it's late for the baby too," Mom said. "This is no place for her to spend the rest of the night. Your dad and I are happy to watch her."

"Thank you," Thorn said as he adjusted himself in the bed. "We appreciate it."

"Wait a second," I said. "I think she'll be find here."

"Kinsley, don't be unreasonable," Thorn countered.

"We'll just step into the hall," dad said. "Let us know, but please let us know soon. These old bones aren't what they used to be, and I think we all need some rest."

"It's fine," I said, but my parents stepped out into the hall anyway.

"Thorn Wilson." I planted my hands on my hips in that way that drove my husband nuts. "I can handle the baby here for another few hours."

"How do you know that it's only going to be a few hours, Kinsley?" Thorn asked. "They're not going to come in here and magically release me as soon as the sun comes up. I could be here until tomorrow night."

"Then I should be here with you," I said.

"No," Thorn said. "You and Laney need to go home and get some rest. I'm going to need you when I get home, and that means you need to be well rested and refreshed. You can't be exhausted and if Laney is exhausted, it will make everything ten times harder."

"And you're saying I can't handle it?"

"I'm not saying that," Thorn said. "But everybody needs rest... I need to rest too. I can't do that if I'm worried about you and the baby being here. There's so much to worry about in the hospital. What about infections? We know how common hospital-acquired infections are. With your healing powers being subdued... I just want to play it safe. I'd rather not take a chance with your health or with Laney's. Plus, I'm going to need to have some private conversations with Jeremy and my deputies. I know you want to be involved, but you can't be here when I discuss the case with them. You know that, so if you stay here, you're going to put the investigation on hold. More people could die. You don't want that."

"Do you really think it's safe for us at home? There is at least one killer clown on the loose. There might be more than one out there."

"Your powers are back," Thorn said. "Other than the healing thing... I know everything else that you are capable of, and you will be safe at home. You've got Meri there too. You just need to lock all the doors, lock all the windows, and make sure that your protection spells and wards are in place. You know they are. And I'll make sure that a deputy drives down our street at least once every hour. You can also have your parents stay with you."

I wanted to be mad at him. I really did, but unfortunately, he was making perfect sense. Laney and I probably were safer at home with Meri.

"Fine," I said. "I'm only going because you need to rest, and because I want to do what is best for you. If you will be better off with us at home and more able to get some sleep, then that's what I'll do."

"Thank you," Thorn said. "Now, come here and give me a kiss, and let me kiss the baby goodnight."

Thorn and I said our goodbyes quickly, and then I exited the room out to the hallway where my parents were waiting.

"I'm going to take the baby home," I said.

"We can come stay with you," my mom offered, either because she'd heard Thorn or because it was just her way.

"No, that's okay. We've got Meri and all of that *security*. You guys go home and get some sleep. I have a feeling before all this is over, we're going to need your help. I think you guys will feel better if you spend the night in your own house and in your own bed."

My parents reluctantly agreed to go home, but only after I promised to call them if I even had the slightest inkling of trouble. My dad walked Laney and me down to my car. And I drove straight home.

The entire time, I kept expecting to see a clown, but nothing happened. I looked between all the buildings, behind every bush, and around every tree. But it seemed that the clown sightings were happening somewhere else.

When we got back to Hangman's House, I put the car in park and we hurried up the front porch to the front door. I had Laney on one hip and my keys already out and ready to go. I put the key in the lock, turned it, and in a second, we were inside. I immediately threw the deadbolt and without even putting Laney down, I checked all of the first-floor windows and the back door.

"What are you doing?" Meri asked as he came sauntering down the stairs from the second floor.

"I'm checking all the locks and windows," I said. "Thorn's okay, by the way. But, there have been multiple sightings of these clowns, and there was another stabbing. At least I have you here, so I know there's nobody in the house."

"Nope," Meri said, and licked his paw. "There's nobody here but me. I haven't seen anybody outside either. But creepy clowns sound just delightful. I'll patrol outside."

"No," I protested. "I don't want you going outside to patrol. I don't want to risk unlocking the doors to open and close them. I also don't want you out there walking around. Nobody has even considered that these clowns could be paranormal or demonic in nature. It's better to just stay inside where the sigils can protect us all."

"You forget who I am," Meri said. "No killer clown is a match for me."

"I know that," I replied. "But I would feel better if you were in here with me. I will have Laney sleep in her playpen down here and I'm gonna stay on the couch."

"Do you think you'd be safer up in the attic?" Meri asked, but his attitude was sarcastic. He thought I was being overly paranoid. I could tell by his snarky tone.

"You're hilarious," I retorted. "I'll feel better down here. That way if anyone is lurking outside, I'll know about it right away. Also, Thorn said one of his deputies will drive by every hour."

"Whatever," Meri said. "I guess I will just roam the perimeter inside and check all the windows to keep lookout."

"Thank you," I said. "I really appreciate it. I also feel better with you here."

"Don't make it weird," Meri snarked.

After that, I got Laney set up in the playpen with her pillow, blanket, and favorite stuffed animal, and she was out like a light. But that was to be expected because it was way past her bedtime.

I grabbed a couple blankets and another pillow for myself from the linen closet and set up the sofa. But sleep was elusive. My mind was racing, and every little noise outside made me jump. I looked out the window at least ten times before I decided that I was probably being ridiculous. But I would never admit that to Meri. I got my laptop and found one of my favorite comfort movies. I figured if nothing else, I could rest while I watched that. Wouldn't you know it? I was asleep within the first ten minutes.

Chapter Five

The next morning, I was woken by the sound of someone gently rapping at my front door. "It's not a clown," Meri said as he jumped out of the front window. "Well, okay, it is a clown. She's just not dangerous."

"What do you mean?" I asked as I stretched and sat up.

"It's Reggie," Meri said. "When's breakfast?"

"Give me a second," I said and looked over at Laney. She'd just woken up too and rubbed her eyes with her tiny fists.

Before I answered the door, I plucked Laney out of the playpen. She rested her head on my shoulder, and I made my way across the living room to the front door. "You're my hero," I said when I opened it and saw that Reggie had brought coffee and breakfast from Viv's place. "Please come in."

"I figured you would need the help," Reggie said. "So, we'll start with coffee and breakfast, and then you can put me to work doing whatever you need, sister," she said. "I can help with Laney. I can do housework. Anything you need."

"Thank you," I replied. "I have a feeling my parents will be here at some point today, but it's good to have you here too."

"I do have a confession to make," Reggie said. "Jeremy spent most of the night up at the hospital with Thorn, so I have no idea what's going on. I've gotten little bits and snippets about clowns? Stuff I've overheard too."

"Yes, it is clowns. I'm assuming that's who attacked Thorn after he went to a call concerning people seeing a clown. He doesn't know for sure, but that's what it's gotta be. And another stabbing came into the hospital while he was in the ER," I said. "The guy looked like he'd been sliced and diced, Reggie. The worst part was, he had a balloon tied around his wrist."

"Oh, man," Reggie said. "Well, do you want me to get Laney changed and dressed? Or, do want me to go in the kitchen and get our breakfast set up?"

"You can go get the kitchen set up," I replied. "Do you have anything in that bag for Meri?"

"Of course, Viv put a double serving of bacon in a little white paper bag for him. She said he'd never forgive her if she didn't include his breakfast."

"That's true," I replied with a chuckle. "Okay, well, feed him first because he's acting like he's dying."

"Hey, I'm right here," Meri groused. "But I am dying..."

"Come on, cat," Reggie said. "Let's get your breakfast so you don't die."

Once I had Laney changed and dressed in a fresh onesie, I brought her in the kitchen and put her in the highchair. Viv had included a croissant for her, so I tore it up into little pieces and gave it to her with some berries and turkey meat. She set to

95

work feeding herself the little pieces of food, and I sat down at the table with Reggie and took a long, satisfying drink of the perfectly hot coffee. "Hazelnut latte," I said with a sigh. "Thank you so much."

"You're most welcome, but there's more."

"There's more?" I asked. "You got more food or coffee?" I didn't see more coffee...

"No, I overheard something while I was waiting in line at Viv's. It was about the clowns and the murders, or the attempted murders. Did the guy in the ER make it?"

"I don't know," I replied. "I'll talk to Thorn about it later today."

"Okay, so there was a lady at Viv's this morning talking about her son telling stories. She seemed convinced that he was just making it up because of something he saw on a scary movie. But she said he saw a clown in the woods behind their house and the kid said the clown tried to lure him out with balloons and candy. She also said that once it was daylight, she went out and checked the tree line where the kid saw the clown. She found a popped balloon, some candy wrappers, and cigarette butts."

"And she still thought the kid was making it up?" I asked.

"I don't know what was up with her," Reggie said. "Maybe she was just dismissing it because she was too afraid or something? She also mentioned something about it possibly being teenagers being stupid."

"That's what Thorn and Jeremy were talking about last night, I think. They thought maybe it was just teenagers being stupid, too. Ugh, I'm so tired. It's all starting to blur together."

"Yeah, well, she thought that maybe it was just teens messing around and that blended together with her kid's imagination. I don't know though, Kinsley. The whole thing sounds super creepy to me. I think I would've been a little more worried about someone trying to lure my kid into the woods at night."

"Maybe I'll have to go take a look myself," I said.

"Kinsley, no. I'm all for you getting involved in this stuff, and I really like to do it too. But don't you think you should stay here this time?"

"I'm hearing that a lot lately," I said. "But Thorn's going to be laid up for a while. My healing magic is all wonky now, and I don't know why. But it means he's actually going to need some time to recuperate. So, somebody's got to do something about this creepy clown murder stuff. We can't just let people keep getting stabbed and if these ghouls are trying to get kids into the woods? We have to do something."

Reggie sighed. "What time your parents going to be here?"

My parent arrived half an hour later. They also had coffee and food from Viv's but no stories of clowns luring children into the woods, so I told them the one Reggie had relayed to me.

"So, you understand that I... we have to go check it out, right?" I asked.

After some negotiation and a promise that I would call Dorian and have him meet us at the woods, Reggie and I were off. I'd received a text message from Thorn stating that he had a full day of tests, doctor consultations, and meetings with his deputies before they released him in the afternoon.

I love you... was his last text to me.

I knew what he was telling me. That I should stay away from the hospital for the day. Not that I'd be in the way... but that I'd probably be in the way.

Fair enough.

Reggie and I were going investigating. Dorian too. He'd practically come through the phone when I told him what we were up to.

"Yes! A million times yes. I'll be there in ten minutes," he said.

"Give us twenty," I said. "I need to stop at the shop to pick up some things."

"I guess I'll have time to brush my teeth, then," Dorian said with a laugh.

"Please do," I replied.

"We're stopping at the shop?" Reggie asked as soon as I was off the phone with Dorian.

I filled her in on Becky and her pleas for my help. She understood, and I wouldn't be long. I had a short list of items, so it was an in-and-out visit. Since it was my shop, I didn't even have to stop at the register and pay. I just gave a wave to the employees covering the shop while Reggie and I were out and headed back to the car.

"What do you have here?" Reggie asked as she opened up the bag and started to go through it.

"It's turmeric, willow bark, and some valerian," I said.

"You're going to give a non-witch valerian root?" Reggie asked. "Like, to eat? Are you sure that's a good idea?"

"It will be fine," I said. "I will ward it so Becky doesn't overdose even if she takes too much."

"You can do that?" Reggie asked.

"I sure can," I said. "Why, do you need some?"

"I mean, I don't need it. It would be nice on nights that I can't sleep," Reggie replied.

"You work at the shop," I said. "You practically... actually... you literally run the place. You know what everything does. Why don't you ask about it?"

"I guess I should have," Reggie admitted. "I'll make sure and ask you next time. What else is in here?"

"There is a black tourmaline necklace with a pain sigil carved into it," I said. "It's to protect the wearer from pain. There is also an amethyst and some rose quartz."

"You think this will do the trick?" Reggie asked.

"I'm absolutely certain that it will," I replied. "There is a small leather bag in there too. I'll have her take some of the herbs as a tea, and the rest she can carry around as a mojo bag on her all times. I think it will heal her."

I felt a brief stab of doubt. It wasn't the same as just using my powers to heal someone, so I hoped that the herbs and crystals would still help. I was sure if they didn't, I'd hear about it. Or, maybe Becky would just come into the shop looking for more help. I'd tell her to come back if she needed additional assistance.

I pulled up in front of the address of the woman Reggie had heard talking about potential clowns that morning. Dorian was parked nearby, and he got out of his car and waved to us as we got out of my car.

The trees were behind the house of a witch that I knew. She was a distant cousin, and if I found something worth looking into in those woods, I had no problem knocking on her door.

For the time being, we snuck through her yard to the trees beyond. About ten feet in, we found the pile of cigarette butts, candy wrappers, and the balloon.

"We probably should have called this in," Reggie said.

"To who? Everyone is basically either at the hospital or patrolling to keep more people from getting killed. I can't imagine they'd bother much with a pile of cigarette butts," I said.

"But there could be DNA on these," Reggie said.

"That's true, but there's nothing tying them to the stabbings. Myrna doesn't even believe her kid about the clown," I replied.

"Myrna?" Dorian asked.

"Yeah, the woman that lives in this house is a distant cousin," I said. "I'm going to talk to her."

"Should we go with you or hang back?" Reggie asked.

"Oh, we're going," Dorian said. He obviously planned on committing every moment to memory to put in a story later.

We made our way around the house to the front porch. I climbed the step first, and Dorian stayed right on my heels. Reggie, on the other hand, stayed on the bottom step. It was probably better that way, because the three of us on Myrna's small front porch would have been intimidating.

I knocked on the door, and Myrna answered a few seconds later. She looked a little shocked to see me, but that wasn't unexpected.

Myrna and I were distant cousins, and we didn't have much contact. But, she definitely knew who I was. As the leader of the Coven, it was an honor for me to darken her doorstep, and there was an obligation for her to be both welcoming and hospitable towards me and my friends.

"Kinsley," Myrna said. "Wow, what an unexpected treat." Her voice was a little too enthusiastic. "Would you guys like to come in? I don't know your friends... But I can make some tea. We could have some cookies. I made some yesterday for the kids."

"No, that's okay," I replied. "I just have a question for you, and then we'll be out of your hair."

"Well, if you're sure," Myrna responded. "What's your question?"

"I wanted to ask you about what you were talking about at Viv's coffeehouse this morning." At that point, Myrna looked over my shoulder and noticed Reggie standing on the bottom step. Her eyes narrowed almost imperceptibly. It was obvious she was annoyed at Reggie for having told me, and she seemed a bit chillier in attitude after that.

"Oh, all that," she said and waved her hand in front of her face like she was swatting away flies. "That was just my kid being dramatic."

"Myrna, I saw the cigarette butts, candy wrappers, and popped balloon out in the woods. I hope you don't mind too much, but my friends and I went and checked it out before we bothered you."

"Oh," Myrna said, and then she rubbed her neck nervously.

"Yeah, like I said, I hope you don't mind that we took a look."

"Oh, not at all. My house is your house, after all," Myrna stated.

"So, you don't think that your son really saw anything? And you didn't think that you needed to report it to my husband?" I asked.

"Well, like I said, I thought it was just my son being dramatic. You know how kids can be. Plus, I heard a rumor that some teenagers were out and about pranking people. Heck, I don't even know if my kid wasn't in on that. You know he's getting to be about that age. He could've been running around with some teenagers trying to scare people too... He won't confess to it, but I did try to get him to tell me.... I just... I don't want to make a big deal of it."

"Myrna, I think we need to make a big deal of it. I think your son was telling the truth, and I think that he and the other kids in this neighborhood might be in danger. You need to keep an eye on them, and keep them in the house until we figure out what's going on."

"Of course," Myrna said and nodded her head yes. "If that's what you want, I'll do it."

"It's more than what I want," I said. "It's what you should do. It doesn't have anything to do with me or the Coven or the family. It's just what you should do as a good mother."

At that point Myrna's cheeks burned furiously with red, and I didn't know if it was shame or anger.

"Is there anything else? Did your son tell you anything else that Thorn or I need to know? It doesn't matter if you think he's telling the truth or not, I need to know."

Myrna seemed to think about it for a few seconds. She rubbed the back of her neck again nervously. "Okay, he did tell me one other thing. Again, at the time, I just thought that he was being overly excitable. I thought that he had the idea of clowns in his head, and that made him see what he said he saw."

"What did he say he saw?" I asked emphatically.

"He said that about half an hour after he saw the clown, there was a man getting into a blue pickup truck up the street. He said the man looked like he had white paint all over his face, and he was wearing a baseball cap and gray coveralls."

"Did he say whether there were any words or pictures on the hats or the coveralls?" I asked.

"No, he said it was a plain black baseball cap and plain gray coveralls," Myrna replied.

"Did he say what kind of truck it was? Or what shade of blue?" I asked.

Myrna turned her head and shouted over her shoulder for her son to come out on the porch and join us. As soon as he was standing next to her, she asked him again if he had seen any pictures or words on the man's hat or coveralls and again the boy said that there weren't any. She then asked him if he knew what kind of truck it was, or if it was dark blue or light blue. The boy said he didn't know what kind of truck it was because it looked like the symbol on the back had been broken off. He also said there was no license plate. Additionally, he said that the truck was a faded blue.

"It might have been light blue, or it might've been because it was an old truck," the boy said. "I'm sorry. I ran to get my phone so I could take a picture of the truck, but the man was already gone."

"That's partially my fault," Myrna said sheepishly. "He was running through the house, and I made him go back and walk."

"It's okay," I said to her and her son. "You've been very helpful. You know how to reach me or my family if you think of anything else?"

"I do," Myrna said. "Please don't hold this against me or my son."

"I'm not," I replied. "But you should start listening to your children."

Myrna turned to her son and pulled him in for a sideways hug, "I'm sorry. Next time I'll listen to you."

On the way home from investigating the woods, I got a text from Jeremy saying that he was on his way to Hangman's House with Thorn. He'd been discharged and Jeremy thought it would be easier to just give him a ride.

I have to go to the hospital anyway... I texted back.

Already on my way. Jeremy answered.

I still need to drop by hospital. Delivery for a shop client. Tell Thorn I'll be home soon. Reggie is with me.

I didn't hear anything after that, but I figured he got the message.

I pulled into a parking space at the hospital, and Reggie and I got out of the car. We made our way up to the sidewalk outside of the emergency room, and I sent Becky a text letting her know I was there. We sat on a bench under a tree and waited a few minutes until she came out.

Once she was outside, we walked a few more feet away from the doors, and I handed her the bag.

"There are some herbs in there that I want you to make into a tea. Drink it whenever you start to feel pain. You can put as much sugar as you like, and you can drink it as iced tea at work if you want to make it ahead of time. Nothing in it is illegal, and I want you to keep some of the herbs in this little bag along with the amethyst and the rose quartz," I said and showed her the little leather satchel. "Keep it in the pocket of you uniform at work, and tie it around one of your belt loops, or keep it in the pocket when you're not working. Wear this necklace as much as you can. You don't have to wear it in the shower or to bed if you don't want to, but I probably would. The chain won't rust."

"Thank you so much," Becky said as she put the necklace on and fastened the clasp. "This means so much to me. Can I make the tea with hot water from the coffee maker in the breakroom?"

"Sure," I replied. "Do they have tea strainer here? If not, you can use a coffee filter tied with a rubber band or a piece of string."

"That's an amazing idea," Becky replied. "I will do that soon as we're done talking. This is my break, and I don't know when I'm going to get another one."

"Well, I don't want to take up too much of your time," I said. "I just wanted to make sure we got these things to you as fast as I could. You can make the tea, and like I said, use as much sweetener as you want. I advise that you use some, even if it's just artificial sweetener. Those herbs can be quite bitter, especially the willow bark."

"I've heard of that," Becky said. "People used to use it before there were things like aspirin, right?"

"Yep, it's been used in folk and herbal remedies for... well, as long as I have had pain," I said with a chuckle. "Wise women used to collect it and prescribe it to the people of their village. The cunning women."

"Isn't that what they used to call witches?" Becky asked.

"You caught me," I said with a chuckle. "I probably would have been in a lot of trouble a few hundred years ago for giving all of this to you."

"That's right," Becky said. "You live in Hangman's House, don't you? Brighton is your mother, and Amelda is your great-grandmother? Does that bother you? Living there, I mean. Given the house's history?"

"Not at all," I said. "It's kind of like... It's kind of like us taking back our power."

"Because your family... You're descended from some of the women who were persecuted in Coventry historically?"

I didn't want to say too much else. I got the feeling that Becky knew we were different, but I didn't want to just come out and say it. I didn't want her putting too much together, even though she had come to me for help. The magical veil was thinner because we were farther away from Coventry, so spelling it all out for her would have been a mistake.

"I love the house," I said. "I don't love everything about its history. But again, it's like taking it back."

"Thank you so much," Becky said and seemed more than happy to drop it. "What do I owe you?"

"Nothing," I replied. "But please come into the shop as soon as you need a refill. Don't wait until you run out."

"Well, I guess I'll be seeing you again then," she said and raised the bag. "Thank you so much for bringing it to me. It's just been crazy around here. The help could not have come at a better time."

"With the stabbings?" I asked because if there was something Becky could give me in return for my magical assistance, it was information. "Is that why it's been so crazy?"

"Yeah," she said. "And we had another one come in just before dawn."

"Another one?" I asked. "Did they have a balloon tied around the wrist too?"

"Yes," Becky said. "It's so bizarre. I have no idea how somebody is stabbing these people, and then tying balloons to their wrists. And nobody notices anything. You would think it would be a spectacle."

"It is very strange," I said. "But I think these people are being lured into the woods. It would explain how the killer is getting away with this and not being seen. I know you can't tell me any patient information, but was there anything else strange about the victim that came in?"

"Nothing," Becky said. "Just a guy out for an early morning jog."

Chapter Six

Jeremy and my dad were getting Thorn settled on the sofa when Reggie and I got back to the house.

"Dad, why don't you and Jeremy go outside and light the grill?" I asked. "And everybody go with them. Please, take some beers, but I need a few minutes alone with my husband."

"All right, everybody out," mom said. "Before I go, though, Laney had a good morning, and she ate a big lunch."

"That's great, she should be ready to take a nap, and soon."

"She is, but she can nap in the baby hammock out on the patio while we have some food and drinks," Mom said.

After that, she and everybody else filed out the back door. I went over and sat down on the sofa next to Thorn. "It's good to have you home," I said.

"It's good to be home," Thorn said. "Do I even want to ask where you were? Do I want to know if you were out asking around about my current case?"

I patted his leg. "Do you want a beer, sweetie?"

Thorn laughed and then clutched his stomach. "Don't make me laugh. Yes, I would love a beer."

"Let me grab that for you. Are you hungry? I imagine the hospital food wasn't very good. If you're too hungry to wait for burgers, I can throw a snack together for you. I'm sorry you're still in pain."

"Well, I'm okay. Just that laughing that kind of smarts," Thorn said. "I had breakfast and lunch at the hospital. It wasn't too bad. Since I was there for an injury and not illness, I got bacon and eggs for breakfast. Lunch was fried fish and coleslaw. It wasn't too bad. And, the beer will help with any lingering aches."

"Well, it's kind of hard to mess up fried food," I said with a laugh. "Guess they're not too worried about what they feed you if you're not in there for a heart condition."

I got up off the sofa and went into the kitchen. I grabbed Thorn a beer and a Coke for myself from the fridge. After popping the top off, I went back into the living room and handed Thorn his bottle. "You want to join our friends?" I asked.

"Sweetie, can we just sit here for a few minutes?" Thorn asked. "I'd like to catch my breath and get my bearings. I just want a few minutes…"

He trailed off. It was then I realized that the attack had damaged more than Thorn's body. He had that look on his face like a lost little boy. It occurred to me that I could try to heal his mind, but I would have to pay the cost for that. Thorn wouldn't have liked that. I'd have to figure out a solution.

Something about the look on his face and the memory of what he'd just been through turned my stomach. I took a sip of my Coke to try to calm it and when that didn't work, I took another.

"You okay?" Thorn asked

"Hey," I protested. "I'm supposed to be worrying about you. I'm fine, just a little stressed about what happened to you."

"I'll be okay," Thorn said. "We'll get through this, and I promise you I'll be fine."

"Just give me a second. I need to use the restroom."

I got up and went into the guest bathroom. After closing the door behind me, and then locking it, I splashed cold water on my face. The queasy feeling did not subside. So, I splashed more water in my face and took a few deep breaths.

After a couple of minutes, the feeling subsided. I dried my hands and went back out to the living room to join Thorn again.

I was just about to sit down on the sofa next to Thorn when the doorbell rang. "I got it," I said. "Don't get up."

Thorn was already getting up. I could tell it was a struggle, too, because he was slower than usual and winced in pain.

"Seriously," I said. "I'll get it. Don't worry."

"With everything going on, I don't really like the idea of you answering the door," Thorn said, but he settled back down onto the sofa.

"Thorn Wilson," I began, "don't you start being ridiculous. I'm not going to stay in this house and not answer the door." I chuckled. "I get that what happened was scary, and I totally get the fact that since it's still happening, it's even scarier. But we're not going that far with our precautions. You are right here. So, I'll get the door."

With that settled, I walked over to the front door and swung it open. I probably should've looked out the front window first, but I wanted to make a show of the fact that everything was okay. Even though I had little reason to believe that... For probably the hundredth time since I'd moved into Hangman's House, I reminded myself that we needed to get a peephole put in the door. Or get some security cameras, if I could ever get them to work.

Standing on my front porch with an endearing smile plastered across his face was Teddy the terrific cabdriver. "Hello," he said and held up the casserole clutched in his weathered hands. "I heard through the grapevine that the sheriff was coming home today, so I brought casserole. It's what my wife would've done. Of course, she would have made a much better casserole than I would, so I must confess that I had my neighbor Betty throw this together. She makes a dang fine tater tot casserole, though, so I'm sure the patient will be pleased."

I wasn't quite sure what to think of Teddy's arrival. He seemed like a really nice guy, but it was kind of strange that he just shown up on our doorstep. Or was it? After all, that was the kind of thing neighbors used to do for each other. When someone was sick, had been in the hospital, or had unfortunately passed away, that person's neighbors will drop by with food and offer their support. So, under the assumption that Teddy was just operating under an older standard of neighborly behavior, I stepped aside and waved my hand for him to come in.

"Thank you," Teddy said. "Where should I put this?"

"Let me show you to the kitchen."

Teddy followed me into the kitchen and put the casserole on the table. He glanced up out the window in the back door and saw my family and our friends in the backyard.

"Oh," he said and blushed a little. "Oh, I didn't mean to interrupt anything. I guess... I'm so rude. I'm sorry... I should've called first. I didn't even think."

"It's okay," I said and patted him on the shoulder. "In fact, why don't you go outside and join in. I'm going to be in here with Thorn for a little bit but everybody's just out there having a beer and getting ready to cook on the grill. You're more than welcome to stay."

It was a rash decision to invite him to the family cookout, but I realized that Teddy was probably at my house because he was feeling lonely. He reached out to help Thorn in our time of need because he needed some company.

"Well, if you're sure you don't mind?" Teddy posed it as a question.

"I'm absolutely sure," I said. "Go on out, grab a beer and hang out with everybody. Once Thorn is done resting a bit, we'll be out too."

While Thorn finished resting, I went into the kitchen and wrapped some corn on the cob in foil for the grill. Before I closed the foil, I covered the corn in butter and coated it in salt, pepper, and chili powder. Once all the cobs were seasoned, I stacked them up on a tray and went back into the living room to check on Thorn. He was getting up, so I went over the sofa to see if I could help him. He waved me away.

"I'm fine," he said. "In fact, why don't you make me useful? I would feel so much better about everything if you guys would stop acting like I'm dying. Give me a job to do. I can't go back to work until the doctor clears me, but I can help around the house."

"Okay. I was about to take some corn on the cob out to the grill. You can help me by taking the chips and dip out. Could you also check with everybody and see if they need more beer or soda for the cooler out there?"

"I can do that," Thorn replied with relief.

We went into the kitchen and I grabbed the dip from the refrigerator and handed it to Thorn. He grabbed two bags of chips from the pantry, and as soon as I had the tray of prepped corn on the cob, we went outside.

"How's the cooler looking?" Thorn asked as he set up the chips and dip on a picnic table.

"Here, Dad," I said and handed him the corn. "Put these on the grill and let me know when you're ready for the meat. I've got burgers, dogs, and chicken in the fridge for sure. I might even have some steak or pork chops. It just depends on what everybody wants."

"I think we will take a little bit of everything," Dad said. "And Thorn, the cooler is about three-quarters full. I'll let you know we need more. Want to come over here and help me with the grill?"

Thorn smiled, and I was glad that my dad was ready to put him to work. He could sense that Thorn didn't want to just sit in a lawn chair while everyone doted all over him.

Although, I would've loved if they would've done that for me. For some reason, I was feeling particularly exhausted. I must have slept worse than I thought worrying about Thorn. Instead of resting, though, I set up an area for Laney to play on a blanket in the grass.

I was nearby when Teddy approached Thorn looking to have a serious conversation. "Sheriff, I've been wanting to talk to you. Is it a bad time? I don't want to bother you when you're recuperating, but

I've got some information that I'd feel better if you knew."

"My ears still work just fine, Teddy," Thorn said good-naturedly. "What is it you want to tell me?"

About that time, I saw Jeremy making his way closer to Thorn and Teddy. He stood back a little bit, but both he and I were within listening distance of their conversation. We were just on opposite sides of the patio.

"Well, Sheriff, I know there's all this weird stuff going on with clowns. And I know your misses called me the other day to come pick up that drunk clown from your daughter's birthday."

"Yes," Thorn said. "But it wasn't that particular clown that was killed. I'm not sure, as strange as it sounds, that he was even involved in any of this."

"That's what I wanted to talk to you about," Teddy replied. "I wouldn't be so sure that he's not involved. I don't want to accuse him of anything, but something was strange that day."

"What makes you say that?" Thorn asked.

"Well, In addition to him being drunk, he was acting kind of... strange that day."

"How do you mean?" Thorn asked. "You're going to have to give me specifics."

"He didn't want me take him straight home," Teddy said. "He made me drive around the block before he let me take into his house on Bay Street. I told him it was gonna cost him extra for the fare, but he had me do it anyway. And then, after the first time, he had me do it again."

"He had you drive around the block twice before he let you drop him off?" Thorn asked.

"Yeah, he did," Teddy said and scratched the back of his neck. "It was a strange thing, right? I asked him if everything was okay, and he said everything was fine. But I got the distinct feeling that everything was not fine."

"Did you see anything weird?" Thorn inquired.

"No," Teddy replied. "And I kept my eyes peeled. As soon as he said to go around the block, I didn't see anything odd. I have no idea what got into that clown."

I'm startled by someone approaching the back from around the side of the house.

"Mrs. Prescott?" Jeremy asks.

"Mrs. Prescott?" I asked the question more to the universe than to the people standing around me at the cookout.

"It's the murder victim's wife," my mom said as she plucked Laney out of the hammock and started walking inside to change her.

I hurried over to the woman. She had a container in her hands, and it looked like a cake inside.

"I didn't mean to interrupt," she said and thrust the container with the cake in it towards me.

I took it. "It's okay," I replied. "I just didn't expect... To see you here?"

"I heard about your husband," she said. " I heard he got out of the hospital today, and I wanted to bring something. I was going to knock on your front door, but I heard you guys around back. So, I came around. I'm so sorry. I thought it would be all right."

By that time, Thorn had made his way over to us. He stood next to me and put one arm around my waist. The gesture almost felt protective. I thought it was strange, but we didn't know who had killed Dewey. The spouse was always the number one suspect until proven otherwise. It seemed, by the way he squeezed his hand against my side, that Thorn hadn't ruled her out yet. Which of course not, because he'd been in the hospital with his own injuries.

On that note, Thorn said something not entirely unexpected. "You can't be here," he said the words as gently as possible. "I am truly sorry about your husband's death, but we have an active investigation going. I hope you can understand."

Mrs. Prescott's face blanched white. Her whole body started to shake, and it was a good thing she'd handed me the container with the cake because she would have dropped it.

"Now, let's not get ahead of ourselves," I said quickly. "It's okay if she stays for a burger. It won't hurt anything."

"Kinsley," Thorn practically hissed my name. But he was wrong, and I was about to tell him why.

I pulled away from his embrace and turned towards him. "Can I talk to you for a second?" I said to Thorn. At that point, he turned back to the still visibly shaking and very pale Mrs. Prescott. "Wait here for one second, honey. Please don't leave. I'm going to have a little chat with my husband. There's been a huge misunderstanding."

We walked a little ways away, and I hope it was far enough that she wouldn't hear our conversation. If she heard, it would ruin everything.

"If there is an active investigation, what could it hurt if we let her have a hamburger and some of the cake she brought?" I asked. "We have plenty to eat. You know my dad is going to go to town on that grill."

"What it could hurt is the effect it can have on the investigation. What if she did it? What will happen to our court case if we were fraternizing with a suspect?" Thorn asked.

"Well, if she's here in a relaxed setting, she might let something slip. Her being here could be part of the investigation," I said. "Did you think about that?"

Thorn's eyes narrowed slightly as he studied me. "I can't tell if you're the kindest or the most devious person I've ever met," he said with a chuckle.

"Why not both?" I asked with a shrug.

"Go tell her I'm sorry, and that she can stay," Thorn said. "Tell her that I'm just out of sorts from getting out of the hospital. After you soften her up, bring her over to me, and I'll make a full apology."

"Sounds like a plan."

But when I turned to go get Mrs. Prescott, she was already making her way back around the house. Apparently, she had decided that we were either too rude or she was too embarrassed to stay.

I went after her calling, "Mrs. Prescott, please come back."

But she didn't stop. I slowed my jog into walk as she approached her car. I stood on the front lawn as she got behind the wheel and pulled away. The best I could do was offer her a wave, but I don't know if she even looked at me.

As Mrs. Prescott drove away from our house, Deputy Liza Strickland and a young man I barely recognized pulled into our driveway.

Liza, Jeremy, and Thorn ended up huddled up out in the yard, while my mom and Reggie played with Laney on the blanket that I set up. It seemed that I had been left to babysit Liza's new boyfriend. He and I sat at the picnic table. I drank a Coke, and he had a beer and ate about half a bag of chips.

Between shoveling chips and dip into his face, I learned his name was Wayne Spacey. Liza and Wayne had been dating for a very short time. The whole thing was new and had that new relationship energy. I could tell, because he kept looking at her, and probably hoping she would come back over to the table. That way, his time with me would be over. We made small chat for a while, but then he said something that made me sit up and listen a little more closely.

"I hope she mentions her neighbor," Wayne said.

"What do you mean?" I asked. I tried not to sound too overeager, but my enthusiasm seems to ignite his.

"Liza has this creepy neighbor. I've always thought the dude was a weirdo, but she thought he was just a harmless old man.

Now, with all this clown stuff going on," he said and waved his hand through the air, "I think somebody needs to do something about that dude."

"You'll have to tell me more," I said and leaned in a little closer.

"This guy that lives down the street from Liza is really into kids," Wayne said.

"That doesn't sound good. What do you mean he's really into kids?"

"He has a lawn chair in his garage that he brings out into the driveway every day when the kids are getting on the school bus, and then he does it again in the afternoon when they get off the school bus. He does it with all three school buses every single day," Wayne said. "He sits there every morning until all of the elementary, middle, and high school kids are on the bus. Then around two o'clock in the afternoon, he brings his lawn chair back out of the garage, and he sits there while all those kids get off the bus and walk home."

"Really?" I asked, but I wasn't quite sure what to make of that.

"Yeah," Wayne said with a disgusted snort. "Liza just said he was a harmless old guy who was looking out for the kids. That's what she always used to believe, but now that all this clown stuff is going on, she's started to rethink it. The whole way over here, she was debating with me about whether she should say something to Thorn and Jeremy about it. I told her she definitely should. That guy needs to be investigated. But she says she doesn't want to make anyone suspicious of the guy if he's just an old man who likes kids. Like he's just being protective of his neighborhood or something."

"I can see how that could be a dilemma," I said.

Later on, while everybody was eating and chatting, and Liza had returned to her boyfriend, I got a couple of minutes alone with Thorn. "Earlier, when you guys were talking, did Liza bring up her neighbor?"

"How did you know about that?" Thorn asked, and I knew that Liza had decided to bring it up.

"Her boyfriend over there, Wayne, was telling me about it. He seems to think that the guy is super creepy and weird, but he wasn't sure if Liza was going to mention it to you."

"She did," Thorn said. "And I appreciate any information that I get that could help with the case, but a guy sitting in his own driveway in a lawn chair is not illegal."

"Don't you think it's creepy?" I asked.

"I can see how people could think it is," Thorn replied. "But from what Liza told me, the guy never talks to the kids. He just watches them get on and off the bus, and then goes back into his house. No one has ever complained about him in the neighborhood. Other than the quirky behavior, no one has any reason to believe that the guy is a bad dude."

"I just think..." I started to say but Thorn cut me off.

"Look, if I find out anything that leads me to believe that there's any chance that the guy has anything to do with the case, I promise I will follow the lead," Thorn said.

"Okay," I agreed. "Let's just enjoy the cookout."

But there was no chance I was going to actually let it go that easily…

Chapter Seven

The next morning, after breakfast, I handed Laney to Thorn, and said, "I'm going out for a while."

"You're going out?" Thorn asked. "Are you going tell me where you're going?"

"I suppose I should," I said. "I'm going to go talk to Liza's neighbor."

"The old man with the lawn chair," Thorn said. "You're going to leave Laney here with me and go talk to one of my deputy's neighbors?"

"Yeah," I said. "I am. You said to put you to work around the house. Well, do you have a problem spending some time with your daughter?"

"That's not what I mean," Thorn said. "You know that's not what I mean. I just don't like the idea of you going to talk to that man is all."

"Well, somebody has to do it," I said. "You can't do it because you're not cleared to work. Plus, I don't think you would go anyway. You don't think there's anything to it, but I do."

"I don't think there's anything to it," Thorn agreed.

"Yes, and because of that, that man's reputation could be ruined. That Wayne guy that's dating Liza seemed really keen on that guy being some sort of creep or weirdo. It's only a matter of time before that starts to get around Coventry. Somebody has got to nip it in the bud. I understand that law enforcement officers aren't necessarily the right people to stop the rumors, but I am."

Thorn took a deep breath. "I get it," he said.

"You do?" I asked. "But you're still going to tell me you don't want me to go."

"Of course I don't want you to go," Thorn replied. "This isn't the 1950s, Kinsley. I'm not going to stomp my feet and forbid you from leaving the house. I'm not going to tell you what to do. You obviously care about this, so Laney and I will hang out, and we look forward to when you get back."

"That's it?" I asked. "Is it okay if I stop by the shop too?"

"Kinsley, you don't have to ask me for permission to go to work. I can't go to work, so I've got no problem taking care of Laney. I feel like you're missing it, though. Do you miss being able to go to work?"

"I wasn't asking for permission. I just wanted to make sure you would be okay for that long. As far as missing work, I do, in a way," I said. "I miss being out in the community and seeing people. I'm just not sure if the shop is where I want to... Go back to?"

"Are you thinking about getting a different job?" Thorn asked.

"I mean, Reggie and our employees are doing a great job running the shop. And I'm very proud of owning it, and of what we built, but I'm just not sure if it's what I want to do. I thought about going to work with Dorian, but Coventry is a small town. We don't really need two reporters."

"So do you have any other ideas?" Thorn asked.

"I've got something brewing," I said. "Nothing too concrete yet, so would it be okay if I just kept it to myself until it's a fully formed idea?"

"As long as it's nothing illegal," Thorn said with a chuckle. "I support you in anything that you want to do as long as it's not against the law."

"Oh, it's definitely not against the law. And I think you and your coworkers are really going to like it."

"Now I'm intrigued," Thorn said.

"Well, hold that thought. When the time is right, we will sit down and work out the details. But for now, I'm going to go talk to an old man about his lawn chair."

I kissed Thorn and Laney goodbye, and went out to the car. I didn't know the man's address, but I did know where Liza lived. It was the right time of day for at least one or two of the school buses to still have to run, so all I had to do was drive over to Liza's house and then look down her street for a man sitting in a lawn chair.

He wasn't hard to find. I pulled up in front of the man's house and got out of my car. "Hello," I called out to him as I walked up the driveway.

"Hello to you," the man said cheerfully. "Is there something I can help you with?"

"There is," I said. "Please don't take any of this the wrong way."

"Oh," the man said with a knowing chuckle. He rubbed his chin and slapped his knee. "I'm guessing you're here because of my little hobby."

"You guessed correctly," I said.

"Did the sheriff send you?" the man asked. "You're his wife, right?"

"I am indeed," I said. "But Thorn did not send me. He doesn't have any reason to believe that you have done anything wrong. Still, I wanted to let you know that your little hobby is making tongues wag. Because of this clown stuff, a man sitting in his driveway watching kids get on and off the school bus has suddenly become something more interesting to some people. I'm afraid those people are going to start spreading rumors."

"Well, my name's John. It seems those rumors have already begun to spread since you're here. However, I can assure you, that I've never dressed as a clown in my entire life. I was Santa a couple of times. I think thirty or forty years ago, I may have even dressed as the Easter Bunny, but never a clown."

"So you used to play Santa and the Easter Bunny?" I asked. "Around here?"

"No," John said. "I lived in the city back then. Well, just outside of Chicago. I moved down here to Coventry after... Well, I might as well just put it out there. I moved down to Coventry after my son died."

"Oh," I said. Suddenly, this school bus thing was starting to make sense, and I felt awful. But I was also glad to come. If my hunch was right, then we could clear John's name.

"What happened to your son?" I asked. "If it's okay for me to ask that."

"If you're thinking that he was abducted, and I sit here to make sure all these kids are safe, I wouldn't blame you. But it was nothing like that. He was sick and passed away. I sit here because I miss having a kid in the house more than anything. I guess I'm kinda lonely too, my wife passed on a few years ago too. But losing our son, and also the prospect of never having any grandchildren either, was the single worst thing in my life. I don't know. I guess sitting out here watching these kids gives me a little bit of joy. They're so full of life. I just like to watch them playing and laughing. Not a care in the world. In the mornings, their entire days are so full of hope, and in the afternoons, they're just so happy to be home. I guess I get to feel a little bit of that too, but I never talk to them. I know what the world is like now, and I didn't want to give anybody the impression that anything untoward was going on."

"I get that," I said.

"So, you'll set the record straight for me?" John asked.

"Yes," I replied. "I'll put the word out that everything is just fine with you. I'll mention that I don't think you have anything to do with the clown attacks. That should clear everything up. People tend to listen to me around here."

"I appreciate it," John said. "And thanks for coming over to chat with me."

I heard a rumbling down the street, and when I turned to look, a school bus had turned onto the road.

"I'll get out of your hair," I said. "It was nice to meet you, John."

"A pleasure to meet you too."

I began walking back to my car, but when I looked over at Liza's house, I saw Wayne sitting on the front porch. He beckoned me over, so I walked down the sidewalk and met him in Liza's front yard.

We stood on the cracked sidewalk under a giant old oak tree. The sound of kids getting off the bus and rushing to their houses echoed behind us.

"So, I see you went and talked to that creeper," Wayne said. "What did the old guy have to say?"

"I don't think he's a creeper," I replied. "It would probably be good, especially since you're dating a deputy, that you not spread that rumor anymore."

"I don't see what me dating Liza has to do with anything," Wayne bristled. "I'm still entitled to my own opinions on things."

"You are, but when you have a significant other of law enforcement, you have a certain image to uphold. Part of the image is not spreading nasty rumors about innocent men."

Wayne seem to think about it for a minute. He scratched his chin and then the back of his neck before letting his arm fall back down to his side. "I don't care what that man told you, I don't think he's innocent."

"Have you ever even talked to him?" I asked.

"Of course I've talked to him," Wayne said. "He's Liza's neighbor. I've had several conversations with the guy."

"Well, did he ever tell you about his son? Did you know that he had a young child that died? That's why John likes sitting there watching the kids get on and off the school bus. He said that losing his son was the worst thing that had ever happened to him. So, after losing his wife too, watching the kids is the only thing that gives him joy."

Wayne appeared to chew that over for a little bit. Then his eyes narrowed, and he stared at John for a second before speaking again. "He said he had a kid that died?"

"Yes," I confirmed.

"He's never once mentioned that to me," Wayne said. "I've gone over there and helped him with a few chores around the house, and he's never mentioned a kid. More than that, I've been in his house. There are no signs of him ever having a kid. There is not one picture of a child in the house. There's no framed artwork... Nothing. Nothing that I would associate with memories of the kid. Not even a teddy bear or... I don't know. That just sounds like a story to me."

"Did you not hear what I said about him losing his kid being the worst experience of his life? Maybe he doesn't want to keep that stuff around? Did you ever think of that?" I asked.

"Then why does he watch the kids?" Wayne asked. "If even having one photograph of his child around is too much for him, then why was he watching all those other children? Wouldn't that be too much for him too?"

Then it was my turn to think things over. I could still understand why Wayne would think that was suspicious, but I didn't think it was. "Grief works in mysterious ways," I said. "Maybe seeing pictures of his own child is too painful, but hearing the joy and laughter from those other kids isn't."

"Whatever," Wayne said. "The guy's a creeper, and nothing you said has changed my mind about that."

"That's fine," I replied. "But you need to keep that opinion to yourself. There's no reason to turn anybody else in this town on him when all of this scary stuff is going on. You could get him hurt. So… Maybe keep that opinion to yourself from now on."

"You'll all see," Wayne said, throwing his hands up in the air. "You are all going to see."

Before I could reply again, Wayne spun around and marched back into Liza's house. With nothing more to do in their neighborhood, I got back in my car, offered John a goodbye wave, and drove over to my shop.

I was feeling too tired to go to the shop. I needed to sit down and have a snack. For some reason, I was getting wiped out easier than normal. I figured it was most likely the stress from Thorn's attack.

Back at home, I found Jeremy's cruiser in the driveway. Inside, he and Thorn were discussing a call Jeremy had just finished up.

I could hear them because Thorn had opened up the front window for Meri. He sat on the window ledge swishing his tail back and forth, while I listened to the conversation without either of their knowledge. Was I being a tad devious? Probably. But I comforted myself with the knowledge that Thorn would have told me what they were talking about anyway had I pressed the matter. This way, though, I got to go out and investigate without any messy discussion or argument.

I stood quietly on the porch and listened to them discuss a high schooler named Billy Boston. Billy had been turned into his school for having a clown costume in his locker. Jeremy had been called in and had interrogated the teenager in the principal's office.

"Jeremy, do you think this kid had anything to do with the attacks?" Thorn asked.

"I don't know," Jeremy replied. "It seems unlikely given the circumstances, but I can't rule it out."

"So what do we do?" Thorn asked.

"The kid is grounded," Jeremy said. "Billy's mom ensured us that Billy will not be leaving the house for the next month."

"School suspension?" Thorn asked.

"Yep," Jeremy replied. "Suspended for a week. Billy is on full lockdown for the next seven days. If the attacks stop, we will know we don't need to look anywhere else."

"It just seems so unlikely that it was a teenager," Thorn said. "Attacking a sheriff and stabbing multiple people. That kid would have to be a psychopath. Is there anything in Billy's history suggesting a mental health issue like that?"

"Absolutely nothing," Jeremy said. "The kid's mother was shocked. She said Billy has never even had to see a therapist before. Billy's a straight-A student and in the band."

"You have to wonder..." Thorn said. "Kids fall in with the wrong crowd, and they do stupid stuff. Especially kids under a lot of pressure. Kids whose parents think they love homework and music practice, but maybe would like to play more video games and hang out with friends."

"We will keep an eye on the kid. If we have another attack while Billy is grounded and suspended from school, then we'll know."

That wasn't good enough for me, so I was going back out. Thorn and Jeremy didn't seem to have any idea I was there. Meri yowled loudly, though, as I started down the steps.

He wasn't too happy about me going out without him again. I didn't say anything, because Thorn and Jeremy would've heard me. So, I tried to make hand signals to let him know to go around the back of the house.

He jumped down out of the front window, and I figured he'd gotten the message. I move quickly and quietly around to the back door and opened it as quietly as I could. Meri darted out, and we made our way back to my car. Within a minute, we were back on the road and headed for my cousin's house.

I had no idea where Billy Boston lived, but if they were having issues with him following the wrong crowd, I knew someone else that was possibly having the same problem. Meri and I drove over to the house where the clown had been seen in the woods, and I parked the car. We got out and made our way up to my cousin's front door.

She answered, and I told her I need to speak to her son. Within five minutes, I had Billy Boston's address, and the promise that my cousin's kid was still staying out of trouble. They hadn't had any more clown sightings after the first one.

As it turned out, Billy only lived a few streets over from my cousin, and that heightened my suspicions. It was possible that the kid had cut through the woods and had been the one standing in the trees trying to lure my cousin's kid out into the woods.

Thorn and Jeremy had said that Billy was a good kid, but smoking didn't really go along with that. Neither did having a clown costume in your school locker. It was possible there was a lot that Billy's mom didn't know about her child.

Billy's parents were not witches, but there was no way Meri was going to let me leave him in the car. So, I let him out and he hid behind some of their bushes. I went to the front door and knocked, and as soon as I had put my knuckles to the wood, I realized that I had not worked out a reason for being there.

I wasn't technically representing the Sheriff's Department, so I had no legal reason to be there. All I could do was hope that Billy's parents knew I was married to the sheriff, so they would answer my questions without too much fuss. Oh, and I had to hope that they didn't report me to Thorn.

I decided the best thing to do was bring up Billy's costume in the context of my cousin's son. At least that gave me a tenuous reason to be there.

A woman in black slacks and a mauve blazer answer the door. She also wore dress shoes and had full makeup with a conservative hairstyle.

To me, it seemed obvious that she had been pulled out of work. The expression of annoyance on her face was further evidence.

"Can I help you?" she asked.

"Yes, ma'am," I said. "Are you Billy Boston's mother. Are you Mrs. Boston? I need to speak with you about Billy. I probably need to talk to Billy as well."

"I am," she said. "Who are you? And why do you need to talk to Billy?"

"My name is Kinsley Wilson," I replied. "I'm here because I heard that Billy had some issues at school today. Something about a clown costume being found in his locker?"

The woman looked back over her shoulder and shouted out for Billy. When she turned back around, she said, "You mean her locker?"

"Billy is a girl?" I asked. But before I even got the question all the way out, a teenage girl appeared next to her mother.

She was a tiny thing. Other than her bright red hair, her small stature was the first thing that struck me. Not only was Billy short, she had to have been under five feet tall, but she had to weigh under a hundred pounds. It was nearly impossible to imagine a teenage girl that small, who didn't have any magical powers, overtaking Thorn. She also would've had to have stabbed several grown men, some of them to death.

"Are you friends with my cousin's son? His name is Astor," I said. "He goes to school with you."

"I know Astor," Billy said. "He's younger than us, but he's hung out with some of my friends a few times."

"So was it you or one of your friends that was hanging out in the woods behind his house?"

Billy's face blanched white. "It wasn't me," she said quickly. "It was my… boyfriend. My boyfriend, Russell. He's why I had the costume too. He asked me to hold onto it. It was stupid. I'm sorry, mom."

"Is that true?" I asked both Billy and her mother.

"The costume was a size extra-large," Billy's mom said. "Would've been falling off of her."

"Does he smoke?" I asked Billy.

I didn't think it was possible for her to get any whiter than she been before, but even more color drained from her face. "Yes," she said, and it came out as a tiny squeak.

"You've been seeing a boy that smokes?" Billy's mom exclaimed. "Billy, I thought we taught you better than that. You have so much going for you, why would you throw it away on a boy like that?"

"Smoking is bad," I admitted. "But let's bring it back around to the fact that this kid was in the woods trying to lure a younger kid out alone. Why was he doing that?"

"It was some sort of initiation," Billy said sheepishly. "Russell and his dumb friends think they're starting a gang. But it's so stupid, because what kind of gang would there be in a small town like Coventry?"

"Initiation?" I asked. "A gang? Like the kind of gang that would attack the town sheriff? And possibly stab to grown men to death?"

"What have you gotten yourself involved in?" Billy's mother asked. "You know what, we're getting a lawyer. This conversation is over."

And with that, Billy's mom shut the door in my face. With nothing else to do, I went back to my car. Meri and I drove home with the weight of more questions hanging over me. Was a bunch of misguided teenage boys the reason all of this was happening? In my mind, it didn't seem to fit.

When I walked in the front door at Hangman's House, Thorn was sitting on the sofa like he was waiting for me. Laney was asleep in the playpen, and Meri darted up the stairs to the second floor. He must have felt the tension in the air.

"Were you waiting for me?" I asked. "Was I gone too long?"

"Where were you?" Thorn asked in a tone that told me he already knew exactly where I had been.

"She called you?" I asked. "Billy's mother called you."

"She did," Thorn confirmed. "Kinsley, what were you thinking? I didn't care about you talking to the guy with the lawn chair because it didn't have anything to do with the actual investigation. Going over to Billy Boston's house and questioning her and her mother? You know that you are interfering in an active investigation, right?"

"I don't know that I would call it interfering," I said. "I'm helping. You can't investigate because you are stuck here until they clear you for work. Time is of the essence."

"And you can't investigate because you're not a deputy," Thorn said. "Kinsley, not only are you putting yourself in danger, but you're putting this case in danger. Is that what you want? Do you want someone else to get hurt? The way I've been hurt?"

"You know that I don't," I said. "And I'm aware that I'm not a deputy. You tell me every chance you get."

"Then why do you insist on doing this?" Thorn asked.

"You know, I thought we were past all this. I thought you understood why I do the things I do, and you weren't going to get mad at me for it anymore."

Thorn sighed. "I don't know what to do with you," he said. "You cannot interfere in an active investigation when people are still dying."

"I wasn't interfering in an investigation," I said. "I was handling a family matter. My cousin's child was threatened, and I had some information as to who it might be. It was Coven business."

"You can't do that," Thorn said. "You can't just wave your hands over everything, call it Coven business, and then expect me to just drop it."

"I can't?" I asked.

Thorn sighed again. "Were you eavesdropping on me and Jeremy? Is that how you got Billy's name? You were here? Wait, I already know the answer to that. Never mind. What did you learn?" he asked.

So, I told him everything that Billy and her mother had told me.

Chapter Eight

"Where are you going?" I asked when I came downstairs the next morning. I'd just finished my shower and found Thorn putting on his shoes. Man, I'd really started to sound just like him. I wondered how long it would be before the two of us started dressing alike.

"I'm going over to the gas station in the new part of town," Thorn said.

"Why?" I asked. "If your cruiser needs gas, can't it wait until you go back to work? Neither of our cars use gas."

"I'm not going for gas," Thorn said. "I just want donuts."

"You want donuts," I said. "Thorn, the donuts at the gas station are not... good."

"I know that," Thorn replied. "But there isn't anywhere in town to get good donuts, and it's ridiculous to drive into the city for that. So, I've adapted. They aren't too horrible."

"What? You mean you eat those donuts from that gas station on a regular basis?" I asked.

"Beggars can't be choosers," Thorn said with a shrug. "Anyway, I'm feeling all right. It will only take me like ten minutes to run over there and come back. Consider it me trying to maintain a sense of normalcy."

"I'll go," I said when I saw Thorn wince in pain as he stood up from the sofa. "I should probably stop at the pharmacy and grab your prescription too."

"I don't need that stuff," Thorn said. "Tylenol is working just fine."

"You're supposed to be taking the muscle relaxers to help you heal," I said. "But if you don't want to take them, then you have to take what I come up with. If you walk around stiff and sore all the time, it's going to take you longer to get better. You need to let yourself rest. Or you need to let me heal you the rest of the way."

Thorn seemed to think it over for a moment. "I'm not taking prescription muscle relaxers or pain pills, and I'm not letting you sacrifice yourself to heal me either. If you come up with one of your concoctions, I'll take it."

"Fine by me," I said. "I'll make you some tea before I go."

And I did. Before I left to get Thorn's donuts, I brewed him a cup of tea similar to what I had given to Becky. I put plenty of honey and a spoonful of sugar in it too and handed it over to him on my way out the door. "Drink all of it," I said emphatically.

"Yes, ma'am," Thorn said and gave me a salute. "I'm going to fix Laney some scrambled eggs and fruit for breakfast."

"Thank you," I said. "There are strawberries in the fridge. She loves those. Just cut them up into bite-sized pieces."

"Will do," Thorn said. "Thank you so much for doing this for me. I appreciate you running out to get crappy donuts for me."

"Anything," I said. "Anytime."

And with that, I was out the door. I drove over to the gas station and truck stop combo and pulled into one of the parking spaces in front of the convenience store portion. As soon as I got out of the car, I could see that there was some sort of commotion. Just inside the doors, there was a crowd of people, and after taking a closer look, I realized they were surrounding a clown. The same one who had showed up drunk to Laney's birthday party. Chuckles looked like he'd gotten himself in some trouble.

"What is this?" I asked as I pushed my way inside.

"I can't believe this fool had the nerve to show up out in public just like this," a man responded.

"It's his job," I said, and I couldn't believe I was actually defending the guy.

"I had a gig this morning," Chuckles said. "But it got canceled when I was in the cab on the way there. I had the cab driver drop me off here so I could get some soda and beer. I was going to walk home."

"Do you really think that was the best idea?" I asked.

"Well, I don't know," Chuckles said and he hiccupped loudly.

"Finish your purchase," I said. "I need to talk to you."

"About what?" Chuckles asked.

"Go buy your soda and beer," I said. "I need to grab a dozen donuts. I'll meet you outside, and don't even think about trying to run off on me. I'll catch you."

Chuckles looked me over. He seemed like he was about to argue, but nothing came out. His shoulders slumped and he took his soda and beer up to the counter. The crowd reluctantly parted for him.

"Why are you helping that guy?" somebody else in the crowd asked.

"Because, like I said, being a clown is his job. He sucks at it, but he doesn't deserve to be attacked out in public just because he is dressed like a clown. I'll make sure he gets home," I said. "He's not a threat."

I could kick myself. Given everything that was going on, was I really going to let Chuckles in my car? Did I even know he wasn't a threat? I reasoned I could hold my own. Especially against a drunken, pathetic clown.

I walked over to the donut case and grabbed one of the cardboard boxes. After filling it with one of each type, I threw the little piece of wax paper away and closed the box. After I paid for the donuts, I walked outside and found Chuckles standing on the sidewalk waiting for me. A car drove by and honked the horn. Another one drove by and someone yelled obscenities out their window at Chuckles.

"Come on," I said. "Get in my car. I will give you a ride home."

"You don't have to do that," Chuckles said.

"I do. I think you're going to get attacked if I don't. And I think it would be a good idea for you to stop wearing that costume out in public until all of this is over."

"Don't tell me shwhat to do, lady,"
Chuckles slurred.

"Just get in the car," I said.

Chuckles opened the door and practically
fell into my car. I sat behind the wheel and
patiently waited for him to buckle his
seatbelt. It took a few tries.

Once he was securely in the passenger
seat, I pulled out of the gas station. The
drive to his house was only a few blocks, so
I had to ask my questions quickly.

"What do you know about these attacks?"
I asked.

"What do you mean?" Chuckles
answered. "Why would I know anything
about them?"

"Chuckles, come on," I said. "Level with
me."

"First of all, my name is Charles Hoogan. If
you're going to call me a nickname, it's
Hoogie. Or Chuck," Chuck corrected. I
was not going to call him "Hoogie."

"Sorry, Chuck. Okay, now that that's out of the way, why don't you tell me what you know about the murders?" I asked again.

"I don't know anything," Chuck said. "Why would I know anything?"

"I was hoping maybe you clowns had some sort of social circle. Or perhaps you had a fraternal organization of some kind?" I asked hopefully.

He laughed and then belched. "No. There's nothing like that. At least, nothing I'm a part of."

"Are you sure?" I asked.

"I wish I was lying, lady. Look, all of this stuff terrifies me. A dead clown is bad enough, but then people are ready to attack anyone dressed like a clown too. It's a mess, and I'm terrified," he said.

"Then why did you wear your clown costume into the convenience store? Why would you do that?" I asked.

"I don't know..." Chuck seemed to think about it and then changed tacks completely. "You know, I tried to get some help. Like, some protection."

"What do you mean?" I asked, but I didn't really want to know. The only reason I even asked was in case he really was the killer and gave himself away.

"I tried to get this domestic violence shelter to let me in," he said. "They had me escorted off the property."

"You can't understand why?" I asked, and I was thankful that we'd pulled onto his street.

"I was abandoned in my time of need," he said as I pulled into the driveway at the address he'd given me.

"Well, it looks like we're here. Good luck," I said.

After he thanked me for the ride, Chuck got out of the car and stumbled up to his front door. I waited for a minute as he fumbled his keys into the lock. Once his front door closed behind him, I pulled out of the driveway and drove home.

Chapter Nine

The next day, Thorn and I were having a late brunch at the kitchen table with Laney when someone rang the doorbell.

"I'll get it," Thorn said.

"Finish your eggs," I said and stood up. "I'm all done."

"I can get it," Thorn said.

"You can get Laney cleaned up when the two of you are done eating," I said.

I opened our front door to find John, the man with the lawn chair, standing on my porch.

"John, what a pleasant surprise," I said. "Did I leave something at your house?" Then I patted my pockets like I might have actually dropped something in the man's driveway.

"No," John answered. "You didn't leave anything in my house. I just wanted to come talk to you. I hope it's not a bad time. I would have called, but I don't have your number. Your house is easy enough to find, though."

"Well come in," I said and stepped out of the way so he could enter the house. "Thorn and I just finished breakfast, but I could fix you something really quick, if you are hungry?"

"No, thank you," he said. "I had breakfast before I came over. But again, thank you so much for the offer."

"Well, how about coffee?"

"Sure. I take it black. If it's no trouble?" John asked.

"None at all," I said. "Why don't you have a seat? I will get us some coffee and be back in a second."

John sat down on one of the chairs flanking our sofa while I made my way into the kitchen. As I was pouring him a cup of coffee, Thorn brought Laney over. "What is he doing here?" Thorn asked quietly.

"I don't know," I said. "I'm about to find that out. I was just getting him a cup of coffee."

"I think Laney and I will join you," Thorn replied.

"The more the merrier," I said. Before I went into the living room, I grabbed myself a bottle of Coke from the fridge. I wasn't really in the mood for more coffee. The butter in the eggs sat heavily in my stomach, and I'd hoped the soda would soothe it.

I walked back into the living room, and I handed John his coffee. He thanked me, and I sat down on the couch. Thorn came into the living room right after me with his own cup of coffee in one hand, and Laney on his other hip. He set his coffee down on the coffee table next to me, and put Laney in her playpen. She sat in there fidgeting with her toys happily while keeping an eye on us. John didn't say anything about it when Meri came into the room and jumped into the playpen with Laney.

"Is that your daughter?" John asked.

"Yes," I said. "Her name is Laney, and she just turned one year old."

"She's a doll," John stated. "You guys must be so proud."

"We are," Thorn practically beamed.

"So, what brings you here?" I asked. I was going to say something about enjoying the company, but I figured it was better to just get to the point.

"Well, I hope it's not too much of an intrusion," John began, "but I wanted to ask you a question."

"Ask away," Thorn said. His foot tapped lightly on the floor giving me the impression that he was, at least slightly, annoyed at the intrusion.

"What I wanted to know is if Wayne Stacy was the one that told you about the rumors about me?" John asked.

"He was," I said, and then realized that maybe I should not have been so forthcoming with that information. I didn't want to start any problems with Liza's neighbors, but John did deserve the truth, in my opinion.

"That's what I thought," John said.

"I thought Kinsley took care of all that," Thorn said. "Does it really matter who started the rumors anymore?" He was putting his sheriff's hat on. Metaphorically, not literally.

"I just like to know who is around me," John said. "I like to know who I need to be careful about. I've had my suspicions about that Wayne guy, and if he's spreading rumors about me, it would seem that I'm correct."

"What kind of suspicions?" Thorn asked.

"It's almost like he's trying to project onto me. One thing he probably didn't tell you, but I've definitely noticed, is that Wayne watches those kids too," John said. "Except he tries to hide it. Also, when he's come into my house to help me with things, he's been entirely too interested in where the pictures of my son are. I know it's because he thinks… Or he wants people to think that I'm up to no good. But there was something about the tone of his voice that told me his interest in my child's pictures weren't entirely… wholesome."

"That's a pretty big accusation," Thorn said.

"Kinda like the ones he's made against me…You know, sometimes men like that date women in law enforcement to cover their tracks. It makes them almost unimpeachable. Because they figure people will think, why is someone who's committing horrible crimes dating someone in law enforcement? The whole time, he's manipulating her. They are doing things under her nose but also behind her back. Dating someone in law enforcement is the perfect cover."

I sat there completely stunned. I didn't know Wayne at all, so it wasn't like I could come to his defense. I'd gotten the feeling that he was off somehow too, but it wasn't something I could put my finger on. Up to that point, I'd only pegged him as a jerk.

"Thank you for coming by and bringing this to my attention," Thorn said and stood up. "I'll walk you out."

The implication being that Thorn was done having John in our house. For whatever reason, the things that John had just said set Thorn off, and he didn't want him in our house around me or Laney. He didn't have to say it, I could feel it emanating off of him. But what I didn't know was why?

I sat and sipped my Coke as I watched Thorn walk John outside. Man, if I could've been a fly on John's car to hear what Thorn said to him before he left. But, of course, Thorn told me nothing.

"I just told the guy to call me if he wanted to discuss anything further. He doesn't need to show up at our house," Thorn said.

So, when Thorn fell asleep on the sofa that afternoon, and Laney was taking her nap in her playpen, I didn't feel bad about the fact that Meri and I slipped out of the house. We drove over to the street behind John's, and I parked the car. My intention was to go into his house, and see if I could find any evidence that he'd had a child. I figured Meri and I could slip in while he sat in the driveway watching the three school buses come and go, and slip back out without being noticed.

Why?

Because the things that John had said about Wayne didn't sit right with me. The problem was, it hadn't made me more suspicious of Wayne...

John's back door was unlocked, and the hinges didn't even creak as I slowly opened it. The whole thing was too easy, but I wasn't about to look a gift horse in the mouth.

The man's house was Spartan to say the least. It wasn't just that there were no pictures of a deceased son around the house, but there were no pictures at all. He'd mentioned having a wife that passed away, but I couldn't find a single photograph of her either.

He was the opposite of a hoarder too. Most of his closets were completely empty of anything but clothing, towels, or cleaning supplies. I finally hit pay dirt in the back of what I assumed was his bedroom closet, though. I found a few boxes, and one of them had a male name written across the top.

Boyd

It was sealed closed with duct tape. The stuff was wound all the way around the lid in several layers. I was digging through my purse looking for something to cut the tape when Meri said, "Use magic, dummy."

I was about to recite my brilliant retort when we heard John's front door open. I froze. Meri froze.

Needless to say, we had to leave without seeing what was in the box. John must have come back into the house to grab a drink or use the bathroom.

I didn't know because Meri and I were trying to shimmy out his bedroom window without getting caught.

We made it, by the way, but I needed a better plan to get to that box. I had to know if it was all the photos and keepsakes of John's son. If it was, then Wayne was definitely my main suspect.

Nope.

Thorn's phone rang during dinner, and he almost didn't answer it.

"It's work," he said.

"Then you definitely should get it," I responded.

"I'm not cleared to work," he said and turned his attention back to the cheese-stuffed meatloaf I'd prepared out of guilt after I returned from breaking into John's house.

"You can answer the phone," I said.

Something wasn't right. I could feel it in the air.

Thorn left the kitchen, but Laney was in the highchair so I couldn't follow him. When he came back into the room, his face was set with concern.

"I have to go," he said.

"What is it? What happened?"

"Wayne was attacked and nearly killed," Thorn said.

"Oh, no. But wait, you're not cleared to work," I said.

"I'm going," Thorn said. "Even if it's in an unofficial capacity. I can advise Jeremy. Or one of the doctors at the hospital can clear me. I feel fine."

I wanted to say that I'd go with him, but why would I do that? I'd have to ask my parents to watch Laney on short notice, and even I couldn't justify it.

"Please call your dad or Dorian to come over," Thorn said.

"I'll be fine," I said.

"Please," he repeated.

"Okay," I said. "I'm sure Dorian would love to hear about all of this anyway."

"Thank you," Thorn said. "Liza is hysterical. She ran out to get burgers and found him stabbed when she returned. I'll be as quick as possible, though."

I kissed him goodbye and tried to call Dorian. I got his voicemail, so I left him a message asking him to come over as soon as he got it.

"I've got juicy gossip," I added as an enticement to get him to hurry.

About ten minutes later, I heard someone pull up out front. I was in the middle of changing Laney's diaper and dressing her in a fresh pair of pajamas, so I couldn't go right to the front door.

Much to my surprise, I heard Dorian walking around to the back of the house. "You're a weirdo," I called out and hoped he heard me. "I'll be back there in a second to unlock the door. Or, you could be a normal person and come to the front!"

I carried Laney into the kitchen and settled her in her highchair. "I'll get your bedtime snack as soon as I let Uncle Dorian in," I cooed.

I walked to the back door and reached for the knob, but something stopped me. Meri came darting into the kitchen as I pushed the curtain covering the window open.

"Oh, my gawd," I said as I saw him.

It wasn't Dorian standing on my back steps. It was a clown, and he had a machete in one hand and a revolver in the other.

"Open the door!" the man screamed, and it took me a second, but I recognized his voice.

John.

Dressed as a clown.

A second after it registered, he used the butt of the gun to break the door's window.

Then, he screamed in agony. The protection magic of the house had shocked him, and he slumped down onto the back steps.

At that moment, something came over me. Something feral took over my mind.

A voice in my head told me he was there for my baby, and my animalistic maternal instincts took hold.

I flung the back door open and set upon him. Meri ran around me in wide circles like he was protecting me inside a circle, and I guess he was. He didn't protest what I did next.

I put my hands on John's chest and did the opposite that I'd done with Thorn in the hospital. If I could heal someone with my life force, then I could take theirs away too. Not something I would have normally done, but I had no choice.

He'd given me no choice. It was him or my baby.

Unfortunate that he'd put himself in that position, but what could I do?

I hadn't meant to kill him. My intention had only been to incapacitate him enough that he dropped his weapons and stayed unconscious until I could get Thorn back to the house to arrest him.

But that night, I rid the world of a predator. I was never able to make myself feel bad about it, either.

Epilogue

"Okay, tell me that again," I said to Thorn over semi-stale gas station donuts and coffee.

"The cyber guys with the state police tracked down John's supposedly anonymous online activity," Thorn said.

"And tell me what they found again?"

"He was dying," Thorn said.

That was why my attempts to incapacitate him had resulted in his death. Well, that and the shocks from the protection spells didn't help either. I wasn't an out-of-control killing machine after all…

"He was dying and he wanted to finally live out his sick fantasies of kidnapping a child… and… I'm just going to leave it there."

"Yes," Thorn said. "And he posted on the board that he thought Wayne was onto him. Of course, the idiot online trolls only encouraged him."

"They encouraged him to kill multiple people first so that law enforcement didn't immediately make the connection between him and Wayne."

"Correct," Thorn agreed. "The whole clown thing was planned out because he knew that teenagers would take it and run with it. He knew they wouldn't be able to resist copycatting that clown thing that went on a few years back, and they'd create a distraction."

"And they did," I said. "Billy and her friends did enough to muddy the waters."

"His plan worked out perfectly until he decided to take our baby," Thorn said with a shudder. "He had no idea that when he stabbed Wayne to draw me out of the house that our house would attack him back."

Thorn didn't know what I'd done. Meri sure as heck hadn't told him. The world thought John had a heart attack when he broke into our house. Thorn thought it was the protection magic that killed him.

"I played a part in that too," I confessed.

"What do you mean?" Thorn asked.

"You know how in the hospital I tried to heal you and it sucked out some of my life force?"

"I do," Thorn said.

"Well, I just did the opposite. I couldn't help it. My instincts to protect Laney took over, and I drew a bunch of John's life force into myself. I only meant to incapacitate him, Thorn, I swear. But it killed him. I killed him."

"He killed himself," Thorn said. "He signed his own death warrant when he stepped foot on our property and threatened our baby. And you. Heck, if I could bring him back, I'd kill him again."

"Thorn," I said.

"Don't speak about this to anyone," Thorn said. "He reaped what he sowed, and it ends there."

"Okay," I said and let out a sigh of relief.

"I can't believe you thought I'd be mad at you about that," Thorn said. "I think I need to soften around the edges a little."

"Couldn't hurt," I teased.

I was about to say something else when my stomach turned over. I felt the color drain from my face, and I had to bolt for the bathroom.

"Are you okay?" Thorn called through the bathroom door.

"Can you grab me a Coke?" I asked between heaves.

"Sure," Thorn said.

When I came out of the bathroom, Thorn was on the sofa with Laney in his lap looking concerned. "It's icy cold," he said. "I opened it for you."

"Thank you," I replied, and I was grateful because my hands were still shaking a little.

"Are you okay?" Thorn asked. "You look like you feel awful."

"Thanks," I said with a chuckle. "I do feel kinda awful, but it's passing. I think it's just because I absorbed that negative energy. It's just got to work its way out of my system."

But, I was wrong. It wasn't the negative energy making my stomach queasy and my body bone tired.

Something new was coming. Something completely unexpected...

Thank you for reading!

© Sara Bourgeois 2021

This story is a work of fiction. Any resemblance to persons alive or dead is a coincidence.

Cover Art by Cover Affairs

Made in the USA
Columbia, SC
23 June 2021

40861989R00104